The Monsters' Anonymous Club

The Monsters' Anonymous Club

Don't Play With Dead Things

J.L. Lipp

ISBN: 1507779194
ISBN 13: 9781507779194

This book is a work of fiction. Names, characters, places and incidents are either products of the author's imagination or used fictitiously. Any resemblance to actual events or locales or persons, living or dead, is entirely coincidental.

Connect with J.L. at www.facebook.com/J.L.Lipp
Email J.L. at MonsterBoyJL@gmail.com

Cover Design and Art by Kevin Richter. www.kevtoon.com

The Eleven Rules of the Monsters' Anonymous Club:

11. Never enter a haunted house by yourself.

10. Never let a vampire know that you know they're a vampire.

9. Never feed a werewolf after sunset.

8. Ghosts don't always know they're dead, so break the news to them gently.

7. Always approach a Zombie from the front.

6. Always check behind your parents' ears before bedtime to make sure they don't have a third eyeball.

5. It's ok to be scared. Just don't let the monsters know you're scared!

4. Never reach under your bed between the hours of 1:00 a.m. and 3:52 a.m., on a Tuesday, Wednesday or Friday.

3. Never play a joke on your parents when dead people are watching.

2. Whenever possible, be nice to monsters because they have feelings, too.

And the <u>most</u> important rule of all:

1. Never, never let adults know about the Monsters' Anonymous Club.

CONTENTS

CHAPTER 1

OF MOTHERS AND MONSTERS

Dead people can be super cranky when they're mad. Just ask Jeremy Bauer, second vice-president of the Monsters' Anonymous Club and first place winner in the "World's Worst Brother" contest. He found out the hard way.

Jeremy should have known better than to taunt the unseen spirits that lurked around every corner in his hometown of Bayview, Michigan. After so many close calls with wild werewolves and vicious vampires and ghastly ghosts, he should have had the common sense not to play with dead things. But common sense wasn't one of Jeremy's stronger traits, especially if there was any possibility to make a joke or get a laugh.

And so, at 9:42 p.m. on Sunday, July 2nd, Jeremy Bauer cast aside all caution to play a little prank on his mother. Unfortunately for Jeremy, he never realized that he was breaking rule number three of the Monsters' Anonymous Club: Never play a joke on your parents when dead people are watching.

"Ouch!" his little sister Kimmy shrieked as he smeared one more tube of fake vampire blood across her face, pushing his thumb so hard into her forehead that it left a small mark.

"Be quiet, you big baby." Jeremy continued to work frantically as he talked. "If Mom hears you crying out like a little kid, she'll know it's all a joke."

Kimmy turned her head and caught a glimpse of herself in the mirror that hung over her dresser. "Gross!" she cried. "I'm not sure this is such a good idea, Jeremy. Mommy was already freaked out by that part of her book where the spirit haunts the little girl."

"Exactly, you dork!" Jeremy was so excited that his face lit up like a pumpkin at Halloween. "That was the part of the book that totally scared her. So when she comes upstairs tonight and finds you floating above the bed, with your face all bloody, the creepy music playing, and the chair hurling itself across the room — she'll freak! It's brilliant, absolutely brilliant!"

"Oh no," Kimmy sighed, "every time you think something's brilliant, it usually ends up being a disaster."

"Too bad we have to keep the room so dark," he said, ignoring her, "or we could film it with my phone and watch it go viral online! Or we could send it to one of those TV shows where they show people doing dumb things and give the stupidest people a zillion dollars!"

"This is stupid all right," Kimmy snickered as Jeremy put one final dab of fake blood on her chin.

"Shhhh ..." Jeremy ordered as he heard the sound of his mother moving around in the living room below. "I think she's getting ready to go to bed. Quick, get in place!"

Throwing her beat-up old teddy bear, Mr. Boggles, off the bed and onto the floor, Kimmy positioned herself on top of two big boxes they had painted black and placed in the center of her bed. Jeremy carefully placed bed sheets over her, creating the perfect illusion that she was floating a good two feet above the bed. It was just like the girl in the scary book their mother was reading.

"This is so uncomfortable," she whispered to Jeremy as he dashed across the room, switched off the overhead light, and turned on the bedside lamp. They had replaced the regular bulb with a black light and the lamp now bathed the whole room with an eerie glow.

Jeremy heard the familiar clicking sound of his mother double-checking the locks on the front door. There was a short pause before the sound of her voice carried all the way up the stairs to Kimmy's second story bedroom, "Jeremy? Kimmy? You two are awful quiet up there."

Kimmy let out two giggles before Jeremy covered her mouth with his hand and gave her a resounding, "Shhhh!" Always ready for a good fight, Kimmy pushed out her lower jaw and tried to bite his hand.

"Ouch, you little brat. Stop that ... ewwww ... my fingers are all covered with vampire blood," Jeremy snorted, wiping his hand across his chest and smearing the fake blood all over his favorite tee shirt.

"Serves you right," Kimmy snorted.

"Kimmy?" The voice was getting louder. Mrs. Bauer was on her way up the stairs. "It's almost ten o'clock, sweetheart. When I open that door, I'd better find you sound asleep in that bed!"

Jeremy could hear the shuffling of his mother's footsteps as she walked up the long staircase that lead to the upstairs bedrooms. He hit the play button on his iPod and the creepy sound of people moaning and wailing came through the Bluetooth speakers he had set up under the bed. The noises traveled through the closed bedroom door and down the staircase. Almost instantly, the sound of the footsteps stopped.

"She heard it!" Jeremy whispered to Kimmy.

"Kimmy? Jeremy?" Mrs. Bauer's voice was trembling. She sounded weak and uncertain.

Moving into position just behind Kimmy's closed bedroom door, Jeremy lay on the ground and scrunched his face in the two-inch gap between the bottom of the door and the floor. He had the perfect view of his mother as she climbed the stairs. He watched as she took one step at a time, moving slowly, her left leg trembling. Then, just as she neared the top step, her right foot caught on the edge and she almost fell backwards. Jeremy held his breath watching as his mother caught herself on the railing, stopped for a brief moment, then continued on.

Jeremy spied for as long as he could, until his mother was only inches from the door, then he ran back to his hiding place behind the antique rocking chair their grandma had given Kimmy as a birthday gift. The doorknob turned slowly, and the door creaked open a few inches.

"Kimmy?" Mrs. Bauer said. But there was no reply.

From his hiding place, Jeremy watched as his mother gently pushed the door all the way open and rubbed her eyes to adjust to the strange light.

He watched breathlessly as his mother looked around the room before her eyes froze on the site of Kimmy floating above the bed, her face covered with blood.

Before she had a chance to move closer, Jeremy pulled a rope that was tied to a desk chair and sent it rolling across the room, straight towards his mother. Just as it appeared the chair would slam into her, the rope reached its length, and the chair came to a sudden stop.

Startled, Mrs. Bauer jumped back, took one more look at her daughter floating above the bed, and then screamed. Not a little scream, but a huge scream. It was the kind of scream that can be heard throughout an entire house, or even across a street, or, in the case of the Bauer family, straight to the Bayview cemetery where a certain ghost was waiting patiently for the opportunity to deliver a very important message.

The scream, so loud that it shook the bedroom windows, continued for what seemed an eternity until Mrs. Bauer cupped her hands over her face and closed her eyes. Jeremy gulped. His face turned red and his blonde hair was now matted down with sweat.

"Mommy?!" Kimmy yelled as she rolled off the boxes and, in the process, fell with a thump to the floor. She scrambled to her feet and ran over to her mother, trying desperately to reassure her that everything was fine, that it had all been one big joke gone horribly wrong. Mrs. Bauer just stood there, her hands covering her face.

"Mommy, it's okay, we were just kidding around! Mommy, are you okay?" Kimmy pleaded.

Jeremy jumped up and ran to his mother. Kimmy gave him a punch on the arm. "I told you we shouldn't have done this!"

Rubbing his arm, Jeremy nodded, "Man, I never thought this would happen. When Dad gets home we're going to be grounded for life!"

Kimmy punched him again. Harder.

"Mom?" Jeremy said, reaching out and gently touching her elbow. "Are you okay, Mom? Really, it was just a joke."

"It was all his idea," Kimmy said, as she jabbed her finger in Jeremy's side.

"Quit poking me, you brat! You had a pretty big role in this, too..."

"Shhhh," Kimmy said, "I think she's coming out of it."

Jeremy fell silent, watching intently as his mother's hands slowly fell away from her face. It was still dark in the bedroom so it took a second for Jeremy and Kimmy to realize that something was now very different about their mother. Her eyes, normally blue like Kimmy's, were now fiery red and her whole face was sunken in as if all life had been drained out. Her olive skin was now dark green, clumps of long brown hair began growing from her chin and from her ears, and most disgusting of all, from inside her left nostril.

"Mommy?" Kimmy said as she took a giant step back to get out of the way.

A nasty smile slowly spread across Mrs. Bauer's now hideous face as she looked back and forth between Kimmy and Jeremy. Then, in a voice that was dark and evil and seemed to echo straight from the pits of hell, she screamed, "Go to bed. Now!"

Jeremy jumped. Kimmy screamed. And Mrs. Bauer just stood there, laughing the most diabolical laugh ever heard in the town of Bayview.

Never taking her eyes off of Jeremy and Kimmy, Mrs. Bauer backed out of the bedroom then disappeared down the long dark hallway. Afraid to move, Jeremy and Kimmy stood frozen like statues.

Kimmy whispered from the corners of her mouth, "is she gone?"

Jeremy shrugged, "I'll give you a dollar if you go check?"

Reaching over, Kimmy gave him a shove. "You're the big brother. You go look!"

Gulping, Jeremy tiptoed to the edge of the bedroom door. Stretching his neck out like a giraffe, he strained to peer around the corner to see if his mother — or whatever she was — was still there. Suddenly, the door began to move by itself, just missing the end of Jeremy's nose as it slammed shut with a huge thud.

Kimmy opened her mouth to scream again, but this time no sound came out. Pulling on the handle with all his strength, Jeremy tried to open the door. It budged open a bit, then slammed shut again. It was as if a much stronger person were pulling it shut from the other side.

"Quick," Jeremy said, grabbing Kimmy and pulling her to the window of the second story bedroom, "we've got to get out of here. And using the door isn't an option!"

Opening the window, Jeremy gazed outside into the night sky. A cold breeze shot past him, causing him to shiver. The rocking chair he had been hiding behind only minutes earlier made a slight creaking sound then, all by itself, started to gently rock back and forth.

Without thinking twice, Jeremy grabbed the rope ladder that was stored next to the window and began to unfurl it to the ground below.

"That's only for emergencies," Kimmy said to him.

"And if this isn't an emergency, what is?!" he yelled back to her as he fastened the ladder firmly to hooks on the inside windowsill.

"Come on," he said, grabbing Kimmy's hand and helping her onto the ladder. "It's just like the time we did the fire drill with Mom and Dad," he said, trying to help her stay calm as she steadied her foot on the top step. They climbed down one after the other, taking one cautious step at a time.

"Wahooooooo," Kimmy yelled as she stepped off the ladder and onto the soft grass of the backyard, "I did it!"

Still holding on to the ladder as he came off the last step, Jeremy was about to high-five her when the sound of a ferocious growl came from above. Looking up, he found himself staring into the glowing eyes of what used to be their mother. Where once she had fingers, there were now only claws. They were long and twisted and came to a sharp point at the ends.

She reached out the bedroom window and, with those horrible claws fully extended, began slowly pulling the ladder up. Jeremy started to run when, all of a sudden, he stumbled and fell forward. His right foot was tangled around the bottom rung of the ladder. Unable to pry his foot free, he was trapped.

Mrs. Bauer began to pull the ladder back up, slowly reeling Jeremy with it as if he were a small fish caught on the end of a hook. Within seconds Jeremy was hanging upside down, his outstretched arms waving wildly as he tried desperately to free himself.

"Help!" he screamed.

Grabbing Jeremy by his upside-down shoulders, Kimmy pulled on him as hard as she could. She was in a tug-of-war with her mother and Jeremy had become the human rope.

"Let go," Kimmy screamed as she gave a ferocious tug. Jeremy's foot came untangled from the ladder and he came flying down, knocking them both into a patch of thorny rosebushes. Jeremy looked up in time to see what was left of the ladder disappear through the bedroom window.

Not wasting another second, he jumped to his feet, grabbed Kimmy and shouted, "Come on! before she comes after us."

"Where to?" Kimmy shrieked as she looked at the painful scratches that now covered her legs.

Jeremy pointed across the alley and two houses down where the familiar light of a computer monitor flickered through David Reid's bedroom window. "We've got to get to David's house. We'll have to use the secret entrance. If ever there was a time we needed the Monsters' Anonymous Club..."

"It's now!" Kimmy yelled, not waiting for Jeremy to finish his sentence.

Never stopping to look back, Jeremy Bauer and his little sister Kimmy ran across the yard, through the alley, and disappeared into the darkness of the night.

CHAPTER 2

THROUGH THE
SECRET ENTRANCE

It was 9:52 p.m. as David Reid, president of the Monsters' Anonymous Club, sat in his darkened bedroom and typed furiously on his computer. The glow from the monitor bounced off his shiny face as he pounded out the last few words in his journal. He had been typing for several hours straight to write down the details of the MAC's recent run-in with a foul-tempered (and very smelly) vampire. He was just finishing his final sentence when the monitor suddenly flickered — the text on the screen began to fade, then became clear again, and then faded once more.

"Must be a power surge," David said to himself as he quickly hit the save button and checked to make sure the document was password-protected. He titled his journal, "Cars to Buy When I Turn 16," instead of its real name, "Confessions of a

Monster Hunter." If his mother ever decided to snoop on his computer, he reasoned, she probably would never bother to read anything with the word "cars" in its title.

David was getting ready to shut down the computer, when all of a sudden his phone gave a ping, the familiar sound of a new text message.

Mom became a Monster tonight. Turned green and real ugly. Good joke went bad. In danger. Coming to your house to hide. Secret Entrance. 2 Minutes . . . HELP! MB7

MB7 stood for Monster Boy 7, Jeremy's code name, and the signal that the Monsters' Anonymous Club was in business and things were serious. Running to his second story bedroom window, David looked out over the backyard to where Jeremy and Kimmy lived. He couldn't believe his eyes. It looked like lightning was striking inside the house! Lights were flashing on and off and the house seemed to be shaking as if it were in the middle of an earthquake.

David could only imagine what was going on inside. Should he go over there? Should he call the police? Should he pinch himself to see if maybe this was all just a bad dream? Ouch! It was real, all right.

Hanging halfway out his second story bedroom window to get a better view, David anchored his waist firmly against the window ledge. Two dark figures dashed across the back yard.

Straining to maintain his balance, David never noticed the intruder who had silently entered his room. Reaching back to grab onto the window frame for support, he found himself instead reaching into the hand of his uninvited guest. David jumped, banging his head on the window frame as he fought to maintain his balance.

"What are you looking at?" the intruder said, sounding more concerned than threatening.

"Mom, you scared me," David snapped, annoyed with her interruption. "What's the point of having a 'Do Not Disturb' sign on your door if everybody ignores it?!"

"Sweetheart, I'm not everybody — I'm your mother. Besides, I heard you typing earlier. Someone has awfully heavy fingers! I was curious what you were working on so late at night?"

Remembering that his phone was lying next to the computer with the text message still visible, David sprinted to his desk, grabbed the phone, and quickly shut it off.

"Nothing," he said and looked away.

David hated lying to his mother, but didn't know what else to say. She had that look on her face like she knew that he knew she knew, that there was something he was hiding. That look was punishment enough.

"Hmmmmm ... Well, whatever it is you're doing by hanging out the window, stop doing it! When I was a little girl I..."

David had heard the story a million times before. "You tried to sneak out of the house by climbing out of a second story window and you broke your arm. I know, Mom! You told me that story before."

"Well, it's so nice to know you listen to me," she said with a sly smile followed with a kiss on his forehead.

"Of course, you never did tell me *why* you were trying to sneak out of the house," David said, tilting his head to one side and flashing his own sly smile back at her.

"And that story will have to wait for another time!" She was about to leave the room when a scratching noise coming from above stopped her in her tracks.

David knew from the familiar sound that it was Jeremy and Kimmy. They had made it into the house, climbed the backstairs, and were now inching their way through the crawl space in the attic. The crawl space led to a trap door that opened in the ceiling of David's closet: the secret entrance that only members of the Monsters' Anonymous Club knew about.

"That's an odd noise," his mother said.

"What's odd?" David said, pretending not to hear anything.

She cocked her head to one side and strained to listen. There was only silence. David looked at her and shrugged his shoulders as if to say "I don't hear anything."

After a second, David's mother turned around and smiled. "Probably just some critters crawling in the attic," she said.

"Yeah," David agreed, "we've got some pretty obnoxious critters in the neighborhood."

"Good-night, dear." She pulled the door shut and was gone.

David rushed to the closet and opened the door. "Jeremy?" he whispered. "Are you there?"

Without warning, the trap door in the ceiling opened and Jeremy came plummeting down, landing on top of David and knocking them both to the floor. A pile of dirty clothes managed to soften the fall and muffle the noise. David had just enough time to catch his breath when, seconds later, Kimmy followed. The three of them, lying in a heap, looked like they'd just been run over by a pack of wild elephants.

Dazed, David sat up, rubbed his eyes and tried to survey the damage to his closet. As he slowly adjusted to the darkness, David began to make out Jeremy's face. The poor kid was white as a ghost. Still, he seemed to be okay. Then David took a good look at Kimmy. He almost fainted. Her face was covered with scratches and dried blood. It looked as if she had just been in a fight with a 200-pound saber-toothed tiger — and lost!

It took a minute for Jeremy to catch his breath before he told David the whole horrible story. Listening intently, David could tell from the tone in Jeremy's voice that he wasn't faking. Having been best friends with Jeremy since second grade, David could tell the difference. This was real.

"I know it was a really dumb thing to do, but we thought it would be funny," Jeremy said as he finished telling the story.

"When I pulled Jeremy off the ladder, we fell into the rosebushes," Kimmy added, pointing to her legs. "That's how my legs got all scratched up. The blood on my face is fake, but the blood on my legs is real. Pretty gross, huh?"

It was all pretty gross to David. For a moment, he felt like he might even throw-up the pineapple and ham pizza he had devoured for dinner only four hours earlier. As president of the Monsters'

Anonymous Club he wasn't supposed to get scared. Yeah, right.

"It was all Jeremy's idea," Kimmy said, giving Jeremy one more punch for good measure.

Jeremy just gave her one of those "you're such a brat" looks.

"Listen, you guys stay here," David said. "I'll run down to the bathroom and get some first aid stuff."

"I'm kind of hungry, too," Kimmy interrupted.

"That kid eats more than anybody I know," David said to Jeremy. It was hard to imagine that such a little pip-squeak could down so much food and stay so little. Once, when David's mom was having a barbecue, Kimmy ate four hot-dogs, two helpings of potato salad, three ears of corn and a huge piece of cherry pie. And it never even gave her a stomachache!

"Okay, okay! I'll grab you some cookies, too. But you guys better be quiet. It's not going to take your mom — or whatever she is — long to discover you're gone. And if she comes over here ..." Noticing the look of complete terror on Kimmy's face, David stopped without finishing the sentence. He wanted to say something comforting, but could only manage a forced smile and a pat on Kimmy's shoulder. They were all scared.

Tiptoeing out of the closet, David tried to be as quiet as possible. Naturally, the closet door made a squeaking sound. It was one of those laws of sneaking around: the quieter you needed something to be, the more noise it ended up making.

David stopped and listened for the sound of his mother's footsteps coming up the stairs to check on him. There was only silence. Maybe she's asleep, he thought. She often fell asleep while reading one of her medical journals.

David's mom was a doctor. She was a kidney specialist and spent a lot of time seeing patients at the local hospital. There's both good and bad things about having a mom who's a doctor, especially when you're running a secret monster club right under her nose.

Oftentimes, late at night, she would need to go to the hospital to see a patient. Now that David was older, she didn't worry about him being alone for a few hours when she needed to go out. She would usually leave him a little note in case he woke up, then head off to the hospital. For David, these late night hours were perfect times for monster hunting.

David was proud of his mother most of the time. She was actually very cool and not nearly as obnoxious about eating vegetables as his friends thought a doctor-mom would be.

Suddenly, David got that sad feeling that sometimes came over him whenever he thought too much about how cool his parents actually were. As great as his mom was, sometimes he really missed his dad. David's dad lived in Northern California where he worked as a computer engineer for some hotshot company called Micro Future 2050. It sounded cool, but he could never exactly explain what they made.

David got to see his father about four times a year. Sometimes his dad would fly to Northern Michigan where David lived with his mom, and sometimes David would get to fly to California. Even though it was fun to fly to San Francisco and hang out in Chinatown, and take a boat to Alcatraz Prison where they used to keep the world's most dangerous criminals, David liked it best when his dad came back to Michigan and hung out at the house.

When his parents were together, they would talk about stupid stuff like people they had gone to college with, or the weather, or, most boring of all, the stock market. It was kind of phony, but at least they didn't fight anymore. A small part of David hoped that maybe someday his parents would get back together. But as he got older — he was now 11 — he began to doubt that would ever happen.

"Yeah, my parents are divorced. Big deal. Lots of kids have divorced parents," is how David would describe it when people asked him about his mom and dad.

The sadness went away as soon as David thought of Jeremy and Kimmy hiding, terrified, in the closet. As he headed down to the bathroom to get some band-aids and first aid spray, he felt a sense of relief that it wasn't his mom people were hiding from.

Suddenly the doorbell rang, causing the hairs on the back of his neck to stand up. It had to be Mrs. Bauer. Who else would be coming over so late? Running to the top of the stairs to give himself a bird's-eye view, he watched helplessly as his mother opened the front door and let the monster in.

"Barb? My goodness, what's wrong, dear?" she said.

Mrs. Bauer stepped in. From David's viewpoint she looked pretty normal. She wasn't green, and there was no extra hair growing out of her nose. He strained to listen to their conversation.

"Lindsay, I'm so sorry to disturb you. Jeremy and Kimmy have run off, and, well, I know how they and David often get into mischief..."

Her voice sounded normal, the same old Mrs. Bauer that David had heard a thousand times before. Maybe Jeremy and Kimmy were trying to pull a fast one on him? Or maybe Mrs. Bauer was playing a joke on Jeremy and Kimmy? Either way, the woman that was downstairs didn't appear to be a monster.

"I have an idea where they are," David's mom said with that knowing tone in her voice.

As she led Mrs. Bauer upstairs, David sprinted to his bedroom where he tried to warn Kimmy and Jeremy. After all, if they got caught in his bedroom, he would be found guilty of aiding and abetting known juvenile delinquents, an act of treason that carried a punishment of severe grounding.

When David came back in, he found Jeremy and Kimmy desperately trying to climb up the closet shelves and through the trap door. Watching Jeremy try to push Kimmy up through the hole in the ceiling almost made David laugh. Kimmy was a little too big and Jeremy was a little too small to make it work.

"David!" his mother yelled from just outside his bedroom. They were busted.

"I have no idea what's going on, and right now I'm too angry to care! Now you and your friends come out here immediately."

David looked back and forth between his mother and Mrs. Bauer on one side, Jeremy and Kimmy on the other. Maybe they could run for it

David thought to himself, his frantic brain working a mile a minute. But how? The trap door was too hard to reach without a ladder, besides, it was a strict rule that no matter what was happening, you should never let adults know about the secret entrance. One mother and one monster now blocked the only other way out.

While David's mother sounded mad, Mrs. Bauer sounded strangely cold and unemotional as she said, "Jeremy, Kimmy, we're going home now." Even David's mom looked a little surprised at how calm she sounded.

With no place to hide, Jeremy and Kimmy stepped out of the closet and started to walk towards the door. Kimmy flinched when her mother — or what was pretending to be her mother — placed a hand on her shoulder.

Helpless, David could only watch as his friends disappeared through the doorway and down the stairs to what had to be a horrible fate. Jeremy glanced back, his eyes filled with terror, pleading for help. David's mother followed them out, still so angry she wasn't even able to look at her son.

Following last, Mrs. Bauer stopped, then slowly looked back at David. She had a grin on her face so evil-looking that it almost made David sick. Then, in a voice that was both deep and repulsive, she whispered the words that would keep David awake and terrified for the rest of the night, "I'll be back to get you - later."

CHAPTER 3

MEET STINKY

David lay awake most of the night, tossing and turning until, completely exhausted, he fell asleep at 5:00 a.m. When he finally woke up, he was surprised to find out it was close to noon. Still groggy, it took him a few minutes to remember that it was Monday, July 3rd.

As the events of the night before began to replay in his mind, David became panicked. What happened to Jeremy and Kimmy? Were they locked up somewhere, he wondered? Or worse yet, were they dead?

David jumped out of bed and began searching frantically for his jeans or a pair of shorts to put on. Why could he never find anything in his room, he thought to himself. He rummaged through a pile of clothes that contained fourteen shirts, three pairs of underwear, eleven socks, but no pants! He was ready to start screaming with frustration when a knock on his bedroom door sent him flying behind his bed to hide.

"David? Are you awake, sleepy head?" It was David's mother. She was holding a pair of just-washed jeans.

His face turning red, David mumbled a faint, "Good morning, Mom" and stood up.

Tossing the jeans to David, she continued, "I just came home for a second, dear, to grab some lunch. I'm working today and need to finish my rounds at the hospital. Can I get you anything to eat?"

David shook his head, startled by his mother's good mood. Besides, he wasn't hungry, just panicked about his friends. But how could he explain that to his mother?

"You know," she continued, "when I get home, we need to have a little chat about last night."

David nodded. Sometimes, when his Mom put off those little chats until later, they never happened. She would usually get busy and forget about it. Besides, it wasn't like David was a juvenile delinquent or anything. For the most part, he was an excellent student whom his teachers described as "very well adjusted, with superior interpersonal communication skills."

"What time are you going to be home?" he asked, almost sounding as if he actually wanted to have that little chat.

"Late. Probably not till after 7:00 p.m., dear. I've got a lot of patients to see in the hospital and with tomorrow being the 4th of July holiday, it's bound to be a busy day."

"I'll make a late dinner for us," David said, confident in his culinary skills.

"Oh, you don't have to. Mrs. Bauer called, she's invited us over for dinner. I told her I would be working late, but that you would be there at six. If I get out early, I'll pop over for some dessert."

David's stomach began to tighten. The only dessert Mrs. Bauer will be serving, he thought to himself, will be slices of kid cake covered with chocolate sauce to hide the blood!

"David, you look white as a ghost." His mother sounded concerned.

"Just practicing," he gulped.

"Practicing?" she looked puzzled.

"The piano. I want to start practicing the piano," David said, trying to think fast on his feet.

"That would be nice," she said. "I just never knew that you played the piano?"

David smiled and shrugged his shoulders. His mother winked, shook her head, and quietly closed the door on her way out.

Grabbing a pair of binoculars, David ran to the window and looked out. Focusing on the Bauer house, he zoomed in on Kimmy's bedroom window. The curtains were closed and there was no sign of movement. At least the house is still standing, he tried to reassure himself.

All of a sudden, David had the uneasy feeling that somebody was watching him. Using the binoculars to inspect every angle of the house, he searched intently for any sign of life. A slight breeze began to blow in through his window, irritating the hairs on the back of his neck. It took a moment for David to realize that the breeze wasn't coming through the window, it was coming from behind him. Somebody was in his room, breathing down his neck! Stay calm, he told himself.

Not listening to his own advice, David let out a yell, spun around and, without even looking, grabbed at the thing that was behind him. Whatever it was grabbed back. They began to struggle, falling to the floor and rolling around and around. David felt like he was fighting for his life.

"Hey, stop it! Stop it!" the thing began to yell out. The voice was familiar.

"Jeremy?"

"Who the heck do you think it is, you stupid jerk?! What are you trying to do, murder me?" Jeremy yelled back, shaking his fists in the air.

"Jeremy, I'm sorry. You scared me. Besides, what's the big idea sneaking up behind me like that?"

"I didn't want to make any noise. Your mom's car was in the driveway. The last thing I want is for her to find me here again."

Catching his breath, David began to calm down and think reasonably. "Listen, we need to convene a meeting of the Monsters' Anonymous Club immediately."

"I'm already ahead of you, Sherlock," Jeremy boasted. "We've got a meeting scheduled in half an hour over at Laura's house. Hurry up and get dressed, we've got a whole lot to discuss."

David quickly got dressed and followed Jeremy out. He wanted to tell Jeremy how glad he was that everything was okay, but he didn't quite know how to say it.

On the way over to Laura's house, Jeremy told David what had happened after they left his house the night before. "It was like she was completely zoned out! She just walked us back home and told us to go to bed. She wasn't possessed like before, but she definitely wasn't our mom, either. This morning, she acted like last night had never happened. She left the house really early with Kimmy."

"With Kimmy?" David was worried.

"To take her to day camp," Jeremy reassured him.

"And then she was going off to work, as usual. I think whatever possessed her last night is gone today. Still ..." Jeremy stopped, unable to finish his thoughts.

"Still what?" David asked, unsure if he wanted to hear the answer.

"It's just," Jeremy stumbled over his words, "I have this strange feeling that it's not over yet. Whatever it is, I think it's watching us and waiting for the right time to strike again."

As they arrived at Laura's house, Jeremy gave David a quick update and assured him that everyone had been brought up to speed about the events of the night before. The Monsters' Anonymous Club was ready for another case.

David had become president of the Monsters' Anonymous Club partly because he was the one that started the club and partly because he was three months older than everyone else. Although he didn't consider himself the bossy type, he liked being president and took the responsibilities very seriously.

The Monsters' Anonymous Club, or MAC for short, had been in existence for a little over a year, beginning when David discovered a family of ghosts living in his house. Members of the MAC helped David deal with this most unusual of problems. After a long series of negotiations, the ghost family finally moved on and, with the exception of an occasional visit, stopped haunting David's house. Since that first case, the MAC met weekly to investigate the strange happenings that plagued their hometown.

The club usually met in the furnished basement of Laura Chen's house. With ping-pong and pool tables, a huge TV, and a refrigerator just for sodas, it was the perfect place to hold meetings. Plus, as Laura was the youngest child by five years, her brothers and sisters were usually either at their part-time jobs or doing homework in their rooms. For the MAC, it was like having a private clubroom.

Laura had moved to Bayview from New York City when she was in the third grade. Her Mother was an administrator at the hospital where David's mother worked. Her father was an English teacher at the local high school. When she and David first met, they absolutely hated each other.

Knowing that they were new in town and that Laura would be in David's class, David's mother invited Laura and her parents over for dinner. The evening was a total disaster. Laura thought David was a rude jerk and he thought she was stuck-up. It took every bit of self-control David had to not throw the strawberry shortcake his mother had made for dessert right in Laura's face. Only after discovering each other's common interest in vampires and aliens from outer space and poltergeists did they became fast friends.

As the first vice-president of the MAC, Laura was fearless. When entering a haunted house, she was usually the first one to go in. Jeremy often joked that David and Laura should be married. It was a joke that neither found very funny.

Heading down to Laura's basement, David noticed big muddy footprints. Either a mummy from the swamps was waiting for them, or Eddie was back from visiting his mother in Phoenix. To put it mildly, Eddie was a bit of a slob. If there was a way to spill something or knock something over or mess things up, Eddie was usually involved. It wasn't worth getting mad about; it was just something you got used to. Austin, Eddie's best friend, was usually around to help clean up the messes.

Best friends since the first grade, Austin and Eddie had a psychic ability to read each other's minds. Once, they were able to communicate this way while Austin was with his parents on a vacation in Maine and Eddie was with his mom visiting the Grand Canyon. Because this ability to read each other's minds, a form of Extra Sensory Perception or ESP, was freaky to adults, they rarely discussed it. Eventually, as he got older, Eddie discovered that he was having a harder time communicating with Austin using their ESP. It was almost as if Austin was uncomfortable using his special gift.

Austin was the quietest member of the MAC. It never failed, every year at the annual parents' and teachers' conference, his homeroom teacher would try to reassure his parents about their shy son by saying things like "still waters run deep." Austin knew that was an adult's way of saying that even though a kid may appear to be unsocial, their mind is working a million miles a minute. And that was definitely true about Austin. Most people couldn't tell just by looking at him, but Austin was a total brain.

As a matter of fact, Austin became a member of the MAC precisely because he considered himself a budding scientist. He believed there was a logical explanation for everything, especially ghosts. He even considered his and Eddie's ESP as nothing more than advanced biology. They simply had bigger brains and could do more!

The minute Austin got the call from Jeremy he began thinking of all the possible explanations for what was wrong with Mrs. Bauer. He was taking notes when Carla walked up to him, a refillable water bottle in one hand, a string of antique beads in the other.

"Oh no, not another list of possible theories," she taunted.

Austin didn't even bother to look up. He was used to Carla's sarcasm. Carla was the complete opposite of Austin. She preferred to think of the world as a magical place, full of unexplained mysteries that people could never fully understand. Always dressed completely in black, Carla was definitely considered an outcast among her classmates. While most of the kids were reading websites about the latest celebrity gossip, Carla was studying about the rituals of the ancient Aztecs.

Carla had always considered herself different from the other kids. When she was little, it would hurt her feelings when other kids made fun of her, or didn't invite her to their birthday parties. It wasn't until she joined the MAC that she finally found a group of people who accepted her. For the first time in her life, she felt like she belonged. Even though she and Austin constantly teased one another, deep down, they were a lot alike. Neither one had friends outside the MAC, and the reality was, they needed each other.

The rest of the members of the MAC fell somewhere between Carla's total belief in the supernatural and Austin's complete skepticism. Having such different viewpoints helped make the MAC successful. For every case that was solved by some logical explanation, there was always a case that simply couldn't be explained unless you acknowledged the existence of the supernatural.

"Those are beautiful beads, Carla. What are they for?" Laura asked.

"They belonged to my grandmother. Just before she died, she gave them to me to carry as an amulet."

"A what?" Jeremy croaked from across the room.

"An amulet," she repeated. "They protect me from evil spirits."

"Gee, those would have been nice to have last night," Jeremy joked, but he really wasn't kidding. Listening more intently than he let on, Austin just rolled his eyes and bit his lower lip.

Surveying the room to make sure everyone was present, David was about to call the meeting to order when he noticed a small patch of fur disappear into Eddie's pocket.

"Eddie," he said cautiously, "either you need to start shaving your shirt or else a mongoose just jumped into your pocket!"

Eddie smiled broadly. "It's not a mongoose. It's my pet hamster, Stinky! My dad found him at work and brought him home." Working as a manager at the local resort, Eddie's dad was always finding strange things that guests left behind.

"I've trained him," Eddie continued. "He can fetch things, as long as they don't weigh too much, that is."

To demonstrate, Eddie unfastened his wrist-watch, tossed it on the floor, and signaled Stinky to go fetch. Sure enough, Stinky hopped out of Eddie's pocket, scurried down his shirt, and, using Eddie's knee and lower leg as a makeshift slide, skated to the floor, retrieved the watch in his little hamster mouth, and then retraced his steps until the plastic watch was safely back in Eddie's outstretched hand.

"Get him to fasten it on your wrist," Jeremy shrugged in his usual sarcastic way, "and we'll really be impressed!"

"I think he's absolutely wonderful," Laura quickly added, while giving Jeremy a dirty look. "But one question," she said. "Why did you name him Stinky?"

"Because he has a lot of gas," Eddie blushed.

With everybody laughing out of control, David tried in vain to officially call the meeting to order. "All right... all right," he shouted over the laughter. "Hamster farts notwithstanding, we've got serious business to deal with here. Someone, or something, has possessed Mrs. Bauer. We've got to get to the bottom of this before something awful happens to Jeremy and Kimmy."

The laughter stopped. Jeremy gulped. "At least Kimmy is safe at her day camp," he said.

"Hey, I'm not afraid of my mommy," the familiar voice cried from the top of the stairs.

"Kimmy! How the heck did you get here? You're supposed to be at camp!" Jeremy's face turned beet red.

"Ah, camp is for kids," Kimmy said, obviously annoyed that her peers weren't more excited to see her.

"But you are a kid ... a bratty little kid!" Jeremy yelled up at her.

Ignoring her brother, Kimmy explained how she so ingeniously escaped that horrible place known as summer camp. "I snuck a ride home with some kid whose mom picked him up after he ate some paste and barfed."

David just rolled his eyes. He knew better than to question Kimmy any further. She was the most stubborn kid he knew. In spite of only being seven, she was determined to be a full-fledged member of the MAC.

"Okay, now that all the members are present," David said, trying to emphasize his irritation with Kimmy's antics, "can we please get back to business!"

Austin jumped in. "First thing we need to do is make sure Mrs. Bauer wasn't pretending to be possessed," he said.

"She wasn't faking it!" Jeremy and Kimmy shouted in unison.

"It's true," David added. "When she left my house last night, there was definitely some other being in her body. It was like looking into the eyes of a zombie."

"Okay," Austin said, taking notes as he continued, "we also need to do a psychological profile on Mrs. Bauer to make sure she's not suffering from a split personality disorder."

"Huh?" Jeremy asked. "I'm not sure I like the sound of that."

"It's possible," Austin continued, "that you and Kimmy scared your mother so bad that she suffered a sort of mental breakdown and now has two separate personalities, one of which thinks it's possessed."

"Would you give it up with all that psycho babble?!" Carla jumped in to the debate. "We all know Mrs. Bauer well enough to realize that she's not some nut case!"

"Thank you," Jeremy said, then added, "I think."

Trying to keep everybody focused, David spoke up. "All right, Austin, you and Eddie continue to do some research on the split personality theory. Tonight Mrs. Bauer has invited my mother and me over for dinner."

"Cool!" Jeremy sounded relieved.

"That will give us an opportunity to observe her behavior and see if we can get any clues from what she says or does," David said.

"If she is possessed, and I think she is," Carla added, "then we'll have to figure out who's possessing her and, more important, why? It all started last night, correct?"

"I see what you're getting at," Laura said, as she looked at Carla. "All this could be tied to some historical event. That's often the case with these types of hauntings. We'll have to research July 2nd to see if anything tragic happened on that date."

David was relieved that the MAC was taking their work seriously. "As much as I hate to say this, Jeremy and Kimmy are in grave danger."

The seriousness of David's tone sent shivers down everyone's spine. "We all have to be prepared to jump into action at a moment's notice, if that's what it takes to save their lives," he said.

The mood in the room became grim. Kimmy's hand was shaking so badly that she was barely able to raise her arm.

"Yes?" David asked, his voice sounded unusually somber.

"Speaking of emergencies, I need to figure out how to get back to camp, before they realize I'm gone and call you know who!"

"Come on," Laura volunteered. "I'll see if my sister can drive you back."

"Nancy's so nice," Eddie said sweetly, causing the others to laugh at his obvious crush on Laura's older sister.

"She's not nice," Laura snickered. "She just got her driver's license and likes to show off, that's all."

"Here." Carla passed her grandmother's beads to Kimmy. "Hold on to these. If anything happens, they'll protect you."

"Thanks," Kimmy offered, then slipped the beads into the pockets of her jean shorts.

To reassure the others that everything would be okay, David tried to smile. Unfortunately, the knot in his stomach was tightening, making a smile almost impossible. Dinner with the monster was only a few hours away and, in all honesty, David was terrified that it might end up being his last meal.

CHAPTER 4

THE LAST SUPPER

"More potatoes, dear?"

David shook his head. "No thanks, Mrs. Bauer. I'm getting full. But they really were delicious!" He stared at her intensely, their eyes locking for a brief moment. She looked like Mrs. Bauer, she sounded like Mrs. Bauer, she even cooked like Mrs. Bauer, but something wasn't quite right. Whatever it was, David couldn't put his finger on it.

Out of the corner of his eye he saw Jeremy and Kimmy. They had barely touched their dinner and were watching every move their mother made, their mouths clenched so tight it would have been impossible to eat even if they wanted to.

"It's a shame your mother couldn't make it. I hope she has a chance to eat at the hospital." Mrs. Bauer sounded almost too polite, just like the mom from the *Brady Bunch*.

"Yes, Ma'am," David said, surprising himself at how formal he sounded.

Standing up, Mrs. Bauer began to clear the table. Plates full of uneaten food filled her hands with more dishes balanced precariously on her forearms.

"When she was in college Mommy used to be a waitress," Kimmy volunteered, obviously proud of her mother's talent to balance so many plates at one time. Speaking too soon, Kimmy failed to notice that Mr. Boggles, one of her old teddy bears, had somehow ended up on the floor. Suddenly, plates and food went flying in every direction as Mrs. Bauer stumbled over the little stuffed animal, lying so innocently behind her on the floor.

Mrs. Bauer let out a small scream as her knee bent forward and her body began to tumble toward the floor. She was going down, and there was no way anybody could catch her. David felt as if everything were happening in slow motion. He reached out, trying desperately to grab Mrs. Bauer and the flying food that was now sailing through the air. A lump of mashed potatoes slid through his fingers, leaving sticky and lumpy potato guts on his hand. After it was over, everyone sat motionless, not sure what to do. Food was everywhere. The once clean dining room now looked like the school cafeteria after a major food fight.

Noticing Mr. Boggles on the floor, ketchup all over his button eyes, Mrs. Bauer screamed, "Kimmy!" Who else would have left a stuffed animal on the floor, David wondered.

For the first time in her life, Kimmy was speechless. David watched as she tried to say something, anything, in her own defense. Only the sound of half-formed words escaped from her lips.

Catching his breath, David jumped up and ran over to Mrs. Bauer. Remembering the first aid class he had taken last spring, he cautioned her not to try and move. She could have sprained an ankle, or worse, broken a bone.

"I … I didn't do it!" Kimmy said, biting her lip to hold back the tears.

"And I suppose he just crawled here on his own accord?" Mrs. Bauer asked in that snotty tone that mothers are allowed to use but kids get punished for.

"Honest," Kimmy tried to explain, "I threw Mr. Boggles away this afternoon!"

"You threw him away?" David felt a chill go up his spine.

"At camp, we were working on a toy drive for kids who don't have a lot of stuff. They told us to go home and see if we could find one toy that we could donate. I was going to donate Mr. Boggles, but then I noticed how ratty and beat-up he had become. It wasn't fair to give him to some other kid. So I decided the best thing was to toss him away. I mean, it's not like I'm a little kid who needs her teddy bear anymore?! So I threw him in the garbage bin, the one in the back alley. Honest!"

Mrs. Bauer just shook her head.

Trying to come up with a logical explanation, David suddenly remembered Jeremy and Kimmy's pet cat. "Maybe Rex dragged him in?"

"I'm sure that must be it," Mrs. Bauer sighed, obviously not wanting to discuss the situation any further.

At that moment David's mother popped in, a bouquet of fresh flowers in her hand. She was in an excellent mood, obviously happy to be done with work for the day. The smile on her face quickly faded when she saw the dining room with broken dishes and food splattered everywhere. Her jaw dropped open as she surveyed the damage then noticed Mrs. Bauer, wincing in pain, on the floor.

"Oh my, Barb, what happened?" She rushed over to her wounded neighbor and immediately began to examine her for any broken bones.

"Oh, just a little accident. You know how clumsy I am, always tripping over things. I'm fine, really. Probably just a little sprain. Nothing that an ice pack won't cure. Ouch ..." She let out a little gasp as Mrs. Reid gently examined her ankle for any broken bones.

"Well, just to be sure, I'm going to take you to the emergency room and get an x-ray on your ankle."

"Oh really, Lindsay .... Can't we just wrap it and keep an eye on it tonight?"

Ignoring Mrs. Bauer's protests, David's mother began the slow process of getting her off the floor and out to the car. All the while, Mrs. Bauer kept saying how she was fine and how she hated to trouble David's mother after such a long day. Mrs. Reid just kept nodding her head while reassuring Mrs. Bauer that everything would be fine.

Helping his mother get Mrs. Bauer into the car while Jeremy and Kimmy started cleaning up, David wondered if his mother had even had a chance to eat all day.

"Do you want us to save you some dinner?" he asked.

She smiled. "Thank you, sweetheart. I'll grab something from the hospital cafeteria. You stay here with Jeremy and Kimmy and help them clean up the mess. I should be back with Mrs. Bauer in a couple of hours."

Making sure no one was watching, David gave his mother a kiss on the cheek. Watching her drive off with Mrs. Bauer, David replayed the evening's events in his head. In retrospect, Mrs. Bauer seemed pretty normal. If she were really possessed, wouldn't she have reacted differently? Maybe the spirit that was possessing her was looking for another victim? What if Kimmy or Jeremy were next? And how did Mr. Boggles, Kimmy's beat-up old teddy bear, end up in the dining room when Kimmy swore she had thrown him in the garbage that afternoon?

David's head began to swim with all the details. Everything was happening too fast. He and the MAC needed more time to figure things out.

Turning to go inside, David began to feel uneasy. Even though his mother and Mrs. Bauer had driven off and Jeremy and Kimmy were inside, he sensed that he wasn't alone there in the yard. Somebody was watching him. But from where?

"Hello?" he called. There was no answer. "Is someone there?"

David turned his head from side to side, trying to make out any movement in the darkness. With the only light coming from the front porch, it was difficult to see. He strained to make out shapes. Was that a man with an ax standing in the yard? No. It was just a small tree that Mrs. Bauer had planted last year. His imagination was now playing tricks on his mind. Picking up his pace, David started to move quickly up the pathway to the front door. He was half way to the door when all of a sudden it appeared from nowhere, freezing him in his tracks. He rubbed his eyes to make sure he was seeing what he thought he was seeing. That's not possible, he said to himself as his brain tried desperately to make sense of what his eyes were picturing. But sure enough, there it was. Crawling out the front door, all by itself, was Kimmy's stuffed teddy bear, Mr. Boggles!

His little bear paws were moving one at time, inching their way down the front walkway. David was frozen in fear. He wanted to scream but nothing came out of his mouth. "Yell," he told himself. "Run! Don't just stand there." Mr. Boggles was closing in. Only a few feet from David, the little bear came to a sudden stop then gradually lifted his head. He was now looking straight at David, his eyes alive with a burning rage. His nose began to twitch as it recognized the scent of raw flesh. The chirping crickets suddenly became silent as the sound of a growl, low and menacing, warned that he was about to attack. His mouth slowly opened to reveal a row of razor sharp teeth. Saliva, sticky and thick, dripped off his lower jaw. He began to move again, faster and faster until he was only a few inches from David. Then, with one more ferocious growl and a sudden lunge, Mr. Boggles was airborne. With outstretched claws and a wide-open mouth, he was flying through the air and heading straight towards David's throat.

"No!!!!" David screamed so loudly that the windows on the front of the house shook. For a brief moment, the world seemed to come to a complete stop. Just as his teeth were about to rip into the flesh of David's throat, Mr. Boggles suddenly dropped to the ground, landing only inches from David's feet. Clutching his throat to make sure it hadn't been ripped out, David cautiously tapped the stuffed animal with his foot. Nothing. Only seconds before Mr. Boggles had been alive, now he was just an inanimate object, lying on the ground like so many other used and abandoned toys.

Taking a deep breath, David reached down and picked up the now harmless stuffed animal. Turning it over and over, he kept searching for a logical explanation. But there was none. Could it be that whatever had possessed Mrs. Bauer had also possessed Mr. Boggles?

Suddenly, Mr. Boggles front paw moved and his head turned back. He was still alive! David tried to throw it down, but the beast wrapped its paws around his hand and wouldn't let go. David flung his arm wildly, trying desperately to get the thing off, but it was useless. Suddenly he heard a voice coming from Mr. Boggles. David couldn't believe his ears. Was he going crazy or was this thing actually talking to him?

"David," the dark voice growled, "remember ... 555!" With one more growl, the head rolled back, the paws fell limp and the scissor like teeth disappeared.

With all his strength, David flung the teddy bear across the yard. It landed a good twenty feet away, resting in the thick foliage of an overgrown hedge.

Trembling, David walked inside where Jeremy and Kimmy were continuing to clean up the dining room.

"Hey," Kimmy said to Jeremy, unaware that David had returned. "Where's Mr. Boggles?"

"How the heck should I know?" Jeremy shrugged. "Maybe he crawled away to go kill some little kid like you!"

"Not funny," David said, as he grabbed a napkin and began wiping off the sticky bear salvia that was dripping from his arm.

CHAPTER 5

555

"What could 555 mean?" Laura whispered into her cell phone, fearful that her parents might hear the late night conversation.

On the other end of the call, David was agitated. "I don't know! I've thought of everything it could possibly stand for, and nothing seems to make sense."

He glanced over at his bedroom clock. It was near midnight and he could tell Laura was getting sleepy. Still, the calmness of her voice was comforting.

"So what happened after Mrs. Bauer got back from the hospital?" she yawned.

"Nothing really. It turns out she just had a bad sprain. So my mom helped her get ready for bed and made sure Jeremy and Kimmy were okay. Then we came back home. My mom was so exhausted she ended up crashing on the couch."

There was a long silence. Laura, in an awkward attempt to change the subject, said simply, "I miss New York."

"Huh?" David was surprised. "What does New York have to do with this? I'm almost mauled to death by a stuffed teddy bear, and all you can think about is New York?"

"New York has nothing to do with this. Absolutely nothing. It's just that we're planning a trip there in August, before classes start. It's all I can think about. I'm going to visit my old acting school and maybe even perform in a scene with Archie Baldwin!"

"Archie Baldwin? You're old boyfriend?" David was starting to feel insecure at the thought of Laura hanging out with her old friends. What if she decided life in New York was more fun than being a member of MAC, and decided to never come back?

"He's not my boyfriend. We just did a bunch of scenes together, that's all. It just so happened that Archie was by far the best guy actor in my class."

"And you were the best chick actor?" David interrupted.

"That's actress! Females are actresses," Laura corrected him. "And we're not chicks! And yes, I guess you could say that I was one of the better actresses in my class."

David just rolled his eyes, glad that Laura wasn't there to see his reaction. Sometimes she could be so full of herself.

"Well, it's been an honor talking with you. I'll look for your picture on the cover of *Teen People*," he joked.

"Laugh if you must," Laura sounded put off. "But someday when I'm rich and famous, you'll call me and beg to be invited to one of my Hollywood parties. And I'll probably say 'David who?' and then I might have one of my assistants send you an autographed picture."

"I won't hold my breath!" David laughed back. "Good night, Mrs. Baldwin!"

"Good night ... peasant!" Click. Laura hungup before David could zing her back.

He looked over at his clock. It was now five minutes past midnight. That meant that it was already July 4th, the day of Bayview's annual Independence Day Parade. David had only missed one parade in his entire life. That was the summer he spent in San Francisco with his father. As cheesy as the parades could be, they were also the place to be. Everybody who was anybody was there. If you we're a little kid, like Kimmy, you decorated your bike and were in the parade. Each of the local elementary schools also had their own float. To actually ride on your school's float, you had to fit all three of the following categories:

1. Be a sixth grader
2. Have a parent who was willing to volunteer a zillion hours (or dollars!) to help build the float
3. Be very popular

David knew that the chances of his ever riding on a float were zero to none. Still, it didn't bug him too much. He had seen enough after-school specials to know that being popular was not all it was cracked up to be. What he really wanted was to someday have a special float just for members of the Monsters' Anonymous Club. He imagined the whole town coming out and calling it MAC Day in Bayview in honor of all the courageous battles that had been fought to stop supernatural forces from taking over their home town.

David had an excellent imagination and he could see in vivid detail all the people pushing and shoving along the parade route, struggling to get a glimpse of the MAC float as it moved slowly down the street. They would be cheering and waving banners and the Mayor would be there to proclaim it MAC day in Bayview. David would receive a special gold medal for his leadership in starting the MAC and they would even rename the high school in his honor.

Now half asleep, David couldn't help but smile. It was these kind of thoughts that kept him going. Over and over again he could visualize himself and the others on the float, waving to all the people in the cheering crowd. A former delivery boy for the morning newspaper, David had gotten to know most of the people in his neighborhood by their names and addresses, and now he imagined them all standing along the parade route, cheering the MAC float on. There was Mr. and Mrs. Anderson who lived at 533 3rd Street and Ms. Burroughs at 537 3rd Street and the O'Connor family from 543 3rd Street and of course old Mr. Crankle, the one customer he had really only seen once, at 555 3rd Street, and who could forget sweet old Mrs. Johnson who lived across the street, and Mr. Henish at ...

David sat straight up. Mr. Crankle at 555 3rd Street? 555! Maybe that's what Mr. Boggles meant? But what could old Mr. Crankle have to do with this?

Around the town of Bayview, Mr. Crankle was legendary. For as long as David could remember, older kids would pass on stories about Mr. Crankle to their younger brothers and sisters. They would warn them to stay away from his house and, for those little kids who needed further convincing, they would tell horrible stories about Mr. Crankle skinning kids alive and cooking them for dinner. Hardly any child made it through grade school without having at least one nightmare about Mr. Crankle.

David, out of intense curiosity, one time asked his mother what she knew about Mr. Crankle. Thinking back, he remembered the conversation as if it had been only the day before. He remembered how the question had surprised her.

"Mr. Crankle?" she repeated, then gave David a suspicious look, before continuing. "I don't really know much about him. He's lived in the same house for as long as I can remember. He's a quiet old man. From what I know, he's been a recluse every since his wife died over ten years ago. Somebody once told me that she had been a schoolteacher down state before retiring here. Why dear?"

"His wife was a school teacher!" David had been astounded when his mother let out that surprising detail. In spite of the fact that they can make a kid's life miserable, deep down, teachers are supposed to like children. You would certainly think that a teacher would marry someone who liked kids, too. But Mr. Crankle always appeared so mean to all the kids on the block. At Halloween time, he would turn his front porch lights off and refuse to give candy to the throngs of costume-clad monsters and ghouls who regularly made 3rd street the hot spot for trick-or-treating.

"Why the interest in Mr. Crankle?" his Mother had asked.

"Just curious," David shrugged, not wanting his Mother to know the gory details of what the kids said about Mr. Crankle. "He's one of my customers on the paper route, only I've only seen him once. And when I said 'hi', he just turned his back and went inside. It was kind of rude."

"Well dear, maybe he didn't hear or see you." David's mother was always thinking of excuses for other people's rude behavior. "Sometimes, old people don't have the best hearing or vision."

Now, almost a year after he had asked his mother about Mr. Crankle, David was beginning to wonder if the "kid eating" stories might be true after all. Even though it was a long shot, one thing was sure, the members of the Monsters' Anonymous Club were going to have to pay Mr. Crankle a little visit.

CHAPTER 6

MR. CRANKLE'S SECRET

It was only 8:00 a.m., but the town of Bayview was already buzzing with activity as people gathered in preparation for the big 4th of July parade. Soon the downtown streets would be filled with thousands of eager bystanders, all of whom had placed their lawn chairs in prime locations along the main parade route. Within a couple of hours they would be slurping snow cones and sucking down cotton candy, keeping themselves contented and stuffed with junk food until the firing of the town cannon at 10:00 am indicated the parade was about to begin.

Having sent an emergency text message to each member of the MAC, David was waiting impatiently for his fearless team to meet him in front of Mr. Crankle's house. As he waited, David scanned the house for any sign of activity. The drapes were drawn and, with the exception of a side window that had been left open a couple of inches, it appeared that the house was tightly sealed.

Three newspapers were stacked on top of one another by the front porch. That's odd, David thought to himself, remembering what it was like when he delivered the morning newspaper to Mr. Crankle. No sooner would he toss the paper on the front porch and turn around to leave, than a hand would shoot out the front door, scoop up the paper, and quickly disappear inside. Maybe Mr. Crankle is out of town he thought to himself? Still, it was unusual that he hadn't put his delivery on hold or, like many of David's past customers would do, arrange to have a neighbor pick the papers up. Besides, from what he knew about Mr. Crankle, he wasn't the type to suddenly take off on a vacation.

"Hey," Jeremy yelled as he peddled his bike up the street. David spun around, gave his friend a stern look and mouthed the words, "shut up!" The last thing they needed to do was draw attention to themselves in front of Mr. Crankle's house.

One by one the rest of the MAC arrived, each prepared in their own way to face the unknown. Only Kimmy, planning to ride her bike in the parade, was absent. Besides, in spite of what she thought, Kimmy was too young to be an official member.

Taking a quick headcount, David asked for an update on Mrs. Bauer.

"She's pretty out of it," Jeremy reported. "Her ankle's swollen to the size of a watermelon and it doesn't look like she'll be walking for at least a couple of days. My dad got home late last night from his trip down state. When he asked her about the past couple of days, she could barely remember anything. Whatever it was — or whoever — well, I think it's gone now."

David nodded. "And what about Mr. Boggles?"

Jeremy's jaw tightened. "What about him? As far as I know, he's still in the bushes where you threw him. There's no way I'm going in after him. Not even for a million bucks!"

"You don't have to," Austin said casually as he pulled out the beaten up teddy bear from his backpack. "I picked him up this morning on my way over."

Seeing the mangled stuffed animal, Jeremy let out a huge scream. Cupping his hand over Jeremy's mouth, David tried to calm his panic-stricken friend. "Shhh..." he warned, "before the cops think some kid's being murdered!"

"Some kid is about to be murdered!" Jeremy said as pointed his fingers in Austin's face.

"I don't understand why you're so afraid of a stuffed animal?" Austin asked innocently.

"You'd be afraid, too, if you were the one who almost got your throat slashed," David snarled. Looking at the now harmless bundle of fabric and stuffing, David blushed as he realized how silly he probably sounded.

"It's possible," Austin continued, "that you just thought you were being attacked by Mr. Boggles."

"You mean you think it was a hallucination?" Laura asked.

"Hallucinations don't crawl into the living room by themselves," Jeremy argued.

"And they don't leave scratches on your arm," David agreed as he pulled up his sleeve to show all the members little red marks that covered his forearm.

"What's a hallucination?" Eddie asked, sounding embarrassed that he was the only one who seemed to not understand.

"It's when you think you're seeing something, but it's really not there," Carla tried to explain.

"Like when people who are lost in the desert are so thirsty that they imagine they see water," Jeremy added.

"That's actually called a mirage," Austin corrected, "but it's the same concept."

"Well I don't know much about hallucinations," Eddie said as he pointed to Mr. Boggles, "but I'd feel a lot better if you'd get rid of that thing. Just in case."

Putting it in his backpack, Austin added, "it's important that we keep all the evidence together. I'm not saying that David wasn't attacked by Mr. Boggles, I'm just saying that there's the possibility that things are different than they first seemed."

Not wanting to discuss it any further, David nodded. "All right, here's the plan. Laura and I are going to knock on the front door. When Mr. Crankle answers, we're going to tell him that my bike broke down and ask him for a glass of water..."

"A real glass of water?" Eddie asked, "or a hallucination?!"

"A real glass!" David could hear the irritation in his own voice.

"Good one!" Jeremy laughed as he gave Eddie a little punch of approval on the shoulder.

David was not amused. "Once we get inside, we'll start talking to Mr. Crankle and see if we can get any clues about what's going on. I'll be wearing the wireless microphone so that you guys can hear us outside. If anything starts to happen..."

"Don't worry," Carla sounded confident. "We'll be there in a flash. You know, I have a very strange feeling about all this. It's almost as if Mr.

Crankle was here right now, listening to everything we're saying."

"Maybe he has a two-way radio wired to the bushes!" Jeremy cracked.

Ignoring Jeremy, David took one final glance around, then called for everyone to assume their positions. Acting like a highly-trained spy team, the MAC instantly scattered, each member heading to their own post. Only David and Laura remained. They each took a deep breath, nodded, and without saying a word, headed up the curved flagstone path that lead to Mr. Crankle's front door.

From their position behind the overgrown bushes that lined the side of Mr. Crankle's house, Austin and Eddie listened intently. As Communication Officers on this mission, it was their duty to track what was happening inside the house and, if necessary, signal the other members to undertake a rescue effort. Austin adjusted the equipment, picking up the thumping sound of David's rapid heartbeat. Eddie reached into his pocket and began to pet Stinky. The little hamster let out a tiny squeal.

"Shhhh," Austin whispered.

"Sorry," Eddie said. "I almost forgot Stinky was with me, he's so quiet."

Through the wire set, Austin picked up the sound of David ringing the doorbell. There was a long pause, followed by Laura's familiar voice. "Ring it again. Mr. Crankle's old, he may not have heard it the first time." Once again, there was the sound of a ringing doorbell followed by a long silence.

"What's happening?" Eddie asked.

"I don't think Mr. Crankle's home," Austin replied.

Laura's voice over the radio confirmed his suspicions. "I think we'd better move ahead to Plan B," she suggested.

"We don't have a Plan B," David replied sheepishly, embarrassed about his lack of planning.

Grabbing the radio and microphone from Austin, Eddie chirped in, "Yes we do."

Laura jumped, startled by the unexpected voice coming from inside David's pocket.

"Hey, you're only supposed to broadcast in cases of absolute emergencies," David scolded as he and Laura quickly headed over to the bushes where Eddie and Austin were stationed.

Ignoring the reprimand, Eddie continued, "we'll send Stinky in to see what's up."

"And I suppose Stinky will come back with a full report?" Jeremy asked, choking back a snort.

"Well, not exactly. But sometimes, when I concentrate real hard, I can see things through

Stinky's eyes," Eddie said, his voice barely rising above a whisper.

"Huh?" Austin asked.

"It's kind of like how you and I used to be able to read each other's minds," Eddie said, recalling the episodes of ESP with Austin.

"That hasn't happened in a long time," Austin said defensively.

"That's because you're not as open to it as you used to be," Eddie tried to explain. "But Stinky, well, he and I have somehow connected telekinetically. If I concentrate real hard, I can see things he's seeing and feel the things he's feeling."

"Amazing," Laura sighed.

David nodded. "Okay, well I guess we have our Plan B. There's a side window that was left open a couple of inches. We'll send Stinky inside and see what he, er... I mean what he and Eddie can see."

Pulling Stinky out of his pocket, Eddie began to prepare his little friend for the big adventure. Rubbing behind Stinky's ears, Eddie reassured him in a voice that was calm and comforting. "Okay Stinky, we're going to send you indoors. Once inside, it's your job to find Mr. Crankle and see what he's up to. This is a big mission, little guy. But I know you can do it."

Staring intently at Eddie, Stinky seemed to be listening to every word. As Eddie finished his instructions, the little hamster let out a high pitched squeal then pushed his nose against Eddie's thumb, as if to say, "Okay boss, I'm ready for action!"

Smiling broadly, Eddie carried Stinky to the side window. The opening was small, less than a quarter of an inch. Judging by the puddles of rain that had pooled on the inside ledge, it appeared that the window had been left open for sometime. Stinky jumped off Eddie's hand and scurried quickly into Mr. Crankle's house.

Eddie closed his eyes and began to concentrate. Within less than 30 seconds he had gone into a deep trance. All the members of the MAC quickly surrounded him, anxious to find out what was happening inside the house.

To David, it looked like Eddie was squinting, his forehead bunched up in a thousand wrinkles. Eddie's teeth began to chatter and his nose started twitching. For a moment, he looked remarkably like Stinky. Noticing the resemblance, Jeremy started to laugh out loud. A quick shove from Laura and he fell into an embarrassed silence.

"What are you seeing?" David asked.

Speaking slowly, as if he and Stinky were in the same room together, Eddie began to report every detail. "We're in the dining room. There's lots of old china and silverware on one side of the table. On the other side, I can see stacks and stacks of letters, tied together by red ribbons. They look very old, as if they had been written several years ago. The paper is all yellow and brittle."

"What do they say?" David asked, his voice rising with anticipation.

"It's kind of hard to read the handwriting, but one of them is addressed to a 'Dear Charlotte' and it's signed 'Love always, Edwin.'"

"You mean they're love letters?" Laura asked as a broad smile crossed her face.

"I guess," Eddie said. "I feel weird reading that kind of stuff."

"Edwin is Mr. Crankle's first name," Carla said, motioning to the mailbox that had a faded "Mr. and Mrs. Edwin Crankle" stenciled on its side.

"Charlotte must have been his wife's name," Laura added. "How wonderfully romantic that he was reading love letters from so long ago."

"His wife's been dead for a long time. He must really miss her," David said, "I wonder if..."

"We smell something," Eddie interrupted, "there's some kind of really nasty odor coming from somewhere in the house."

"It's probably just Stinky!" Jeremy laughed.

But Eddie was serious. "No, it's worse than that. It smells like that time a squirrel got caught in our attic and died. By the time my dad found his body, he had rotted out."

"You don't think something's dead in there, do you?" Carla asked nervously.

"I don't know, but I kind of wish we could get out of here," Eddie answered, his voice starting to quiver.

"Everything's going to be okay, Eddie," David said. "Just tell Stinky to slowly turn around and head back out the way he came."

Still very much in his trance, Eddie continued. "Hey Stinky, come on and turn around now. You've done your duty, it's time to head home for a peanut butter and jelly and cheddar cheese sandwich. Oh no, he's heading toward the kitchen. Oh man, the smell is getting worse and worse. Stinky, time to go. What's that? Wait, I think I see something on the floor, behind the kitchen counter. It's like somebody left their gray sweater on the floor. No, wait. It's somebody in a gray sweater. It's Mr. Crankle! He's on the floor and he's... he's ... he's just like that squirrel! His body is all purple and his eyes ... his eyes are wide open. He's dead! Mr. Crankle is dead!"

CHAPTER 7

DON'T PLAY WITH DEAD THINGS

"**D**ead?" David asked in disbelief. "Are you sure?"

"Come on Stinky ... Hurry up ... get out of there," Eddie's voice kept getting higher and higher as he frantically tried to steer his little friend out of the kitchen and back to the safety of his pocket. Suddenly snapping out of his trance, Eddie cried out, "Oh no ... no!"

"What's wrong?" Laura asked, concerned about both Eddie and Stinky.

"I've lost him! I've lost Stinky. My concentration is gone and we've lost contact. We've got to do something!" Eddie was close to tears.

"I'm not going after him," Jeremy shook his head. "There's no way I want to see some dead guy lying on the kitchen floor."

"We've got to get him out of there!" Eddie roared.

"Okay... okay ... calm down, Eddie. We're not going to leave Stinky behind. He's our star spy. I'll go in and get him," David said, straining to sound composed and in control.

"You?" Laura and Austin asked in unison.

"Yes. I'll just pop open the window all the way and crawl in. Obviously, there's nobody inside I have to worry about." David was trying to reassure the others, as well as himself, that it would be a simple rescue mission.

"But what if Mr. Crankle was murdered, and the killer's still inside?" Jeremy asked.

"Don't be ridiculous," Austin scolded. "Besides, I'm not letting David go in alone. I'm going with him." David was touched by the spirit of friendship from Austin.

"Me too!" Laura added.

"And me too," cried Carla.

"He's my hamster, so I'd better go with you as well," Eddie asserted.

Jeremy's mouth fell open and his face reddened. "Well, it makes sense for one of us to stay here and act as a lookout. I guess I'll make the sacrifice."

"Chicken!" Eddie sneered.

"Listen you tub of lard ..." Jeremy started, but was quickly cut off by Laura.

"Knock it off, both of you!" Laura's voice was forceful.

"We've got to get in there, get Stinky, assess the scene, and collect any evidence. Whatever evil spirit we've been dealing with, it may have something to do with Mr. Crankle's death."

"You think that's what killed him," Carla asked, "an evil spirit?"

"I hope not," Laura added. "We'll have to move fast and get as much information as possible. Once the police investigate, we'll never get back in."

"Who cares about the evidence, I just want Stinky back!" Eddie said, his voice cracking with emotion.

Realizing time was of the essence, it was close to 9:00 a.m., David moved quickly. Taking out the walkie talkies that were always carried on missions — much more efficient for two-way communications than cell phones — David turned the power knobs on and set the channels to seven. As he handed one to Jeremy, he never noticed the flashing of the "low battery" light. With Jeremy's reluctant assistance, the two of them pushed open the side window all the way and David crawled into the house. The puddles of rain water on the inside windowsill seeped into his jeans. Inside, he took a deep breath and was immediately over-come by a stale, musty smell that filled his sinuses and almost made him gag.

Leaning back out, he gave an "okay" signal and one by one the other members of the MAC climbed through the window, leaving only Jeremy to stand guard outside. Each made the same face as they took that first breath of stale air.

"Wow!" Laura said, "this place smells really musty, like it's been shut up for months."

"Stinky? Come here, Stinky!" Eddie called out in a loud whisper, sounding more concerned about his little pal than afraid of what waited around the corner.

Moving slowly through the living and din-ing room, each member of the MAC spread out to search for clues and look for Stinky. Laura and Carla headed over to the stack of letters left on the dining room table. A glass of milk, now spoiled and looking like lumpy cottage cheese, and a bunch of cookie crumbs lay next to the let-ters. One letter was separated from the stack, a small paperweight placed carefully on top of it.

"Based on what's here, I'm guessing that Mr. Crankle must have been reading the letters just before he died," Laura said, as she carefully examined the evidence.

Carla concurred. "Perhaps he was reading the letters and having some milk and cookies, when he needed to get something from the kitchen?"

"Some more cookies?" Laura guessed.

"Or maybe a napkin?" Carla added. "So he gets up, goes to the kitchen and something happens in there."

"He could have had a heart attack," Laura offered, "or maybe it was some kind of terrible accident. Maybe he tripped on something and hit his head on the floor?"

Eddie jumped into the conversation from across the room. "Or maybe Jeremy was right and it was some sort of intruder who killed him? Or, even worse, maybe the monster that possessed both Mrs. Bauer and Mr. Boggles killed him?

"There's so many different scenarios," Carla said.

"But we'll never know until we examine the body," Austin said as he continued to jot down notes.

Noticing the letter that had been singled out by Mr. Crankle in the last moments of his life, Laura read the first few lines to herself. "Everybody needs to hear this," she said.

As she read the letter out aloud, Laura's voice became soft and respectful.

May 17, 1948

My Dear Charlotte:
  I write this letter to you from France. So much has happened over here; everywhere you look there's destruction and loss. It makes me realize that my love for you is the most important thing in life and that, being together forever, is where our souls belong. Each day I caress the wedding ring that binds us together and from it, gather the strength to go on. Please know, that even though we are thousands of miles apart, you are always in my heart and will be so forever. Even as time moves on and someday we find ourselves separated between heaven and earth, please know that such separations will only be momentary. For you are the love of my life for all eternity.

Love Always, Edwin

There was a moment of silence. Laura sniffed and rubbed a tear from the corner of her eye.

Even Austin, who was always reluctant to share his feelings with others, appeared to be moved by the letter. "Look at this," he said as he picked up a yellowed clipping from the local newspaper lying almost unnoticed under the stack of letters. "It's a copy of Mrs. Crankle's obituary from 2004. It's even got a small picture of her," he said, his voice cracking slightly.

"Look at what a nice smile she had," Laura said. "She looks just like my grandmother who lives in upstate New York."

"It looks like Mrs. Crankle died over ten years ago and poor Mr. Crankle had been heartbroken ever since," David said, trying to make sense of all the pieces.

"But that still doesn't explain what killed him," Austin added. "I think it's time we went and examined the body!"

Eddie gulped. "It's one thing to see a dead body through Stinky's eyes, but to see it for real? I think I'm going to barf."

"Stay calm, Eddie." David tried to quiet his friend down. "We're all in this together. Remember everybody, when we do go in the kitchen, don't get too close to the body. Dead things can carry all kinds of diseases." The others stared at David, as looks of disgust spread across their faces.

"Just be careful, that's all," David said as he slowly led the group into the kitchen. Almost immediately he was overcome by the foul smell that filled the room. It was like the time the power had gone out for three days and all the food in the refrigerator had spoiled. Instinctively, he covered his mouth and nose with his hands.

His notepad and pen firmly in hand, Austin started to take notes. Speaking out loud as he wrote, he said, "it appears as though the victim has been dead for a couple of days. His body, lying face down on the kitchen floor, is in an early stage of decay. Although it's hard to tell, I see no evidence of external wounds on the body. There appears to be no evidence of forced entry into the house or of foul play."

"Wow!" Carla added, sounding more fascinated than frightened. "I've never seen a dead person before. It's hard to explain, but he looks almost calm."

"Well, he may look calm," David said, "but something connected to this house is angry, and it's still out there. And I have a feeling..."

"Ahhhhh ..." Eddie let out a scream that almost knocked the notepad and pen out of Austin's hands.

"What?" David said, lowering his voice to try and calm Eddie down.

"He moved! Mr. Crankle moved!" Eddie said as he frantically pointed at Mr. Crankle's body.

"Where, I don't see anything?" David said as he stared intently at Mr. Crankle, looking for any signs of life.

"I saw it too," Laura suddenly whispered. "His sweater moved up and down, like he's still breathing!"

"Impossible," Austin jumped in. "There's no way he's still...ahhhhh, he moved! I saw it!"

This time, they all saw it. Mr. Crankle's sweater was actually moving up and down.

"Mr. Crankle?" David asked, slowly bending over. "Are you okay, sir? Mr. Crankle, sir?"

Trembling, David reached down, his hand inches from Mr. Crankle's left shoulder. "Mr. Crankle?" he called softly, but there was no reply.

Suddenly, the neck of Mr. Crankle's sweater flew open and out popped Stinky, his little nose twitching with excitement.

"Stinky!" Eddie cried. "Mr. Crankle wasn't alive, it was just you crawling under his sweater." Hearing the sound of Eddie's voice, Stinky ran down Mr. Crankle's back and over to Eddie's outstretched hand.

"What's that in his mouth?" Laura asked, noticing a small piece of metal sticking out of Stinky's jowls.

"Open up, boy," Eddie coaxed as he gently petted Stinky's neck.

Stinky cocked his head to one side, gave his little hamster butt a big shake, then opened his mouth to let his newly found treasure drop gently into Eddie's hand.

"It's a ring!" Eddie exclaimed.

"That's not just any ring, it's a wedding ring," Laura said as she stepped in closer to examine the small golden band that lay in Eddie's hand.

Just as David reached out to examine the ring, a gust of freezing wind shot through the house, slamming the kitchen door shut with a bang, and knocking the ring from Eddie's hand. The ring bounced twice on the floor then rolled across the floor before coming to a stop just in front of Mr. Crankle's hand.

In the front yard, Jeremy was pacing nervously. "What's taking you guys so long?" he said, his voice barely rising above a whisper. Picking up the radio, he pushed the call button and began, "Big Charlie, this is Monster Boy 7, do you copy?"

There was no reply.

Jeremy repeated his call before noticing that the radio wasn't working. He flipped the "on/off" switch several times, but to no avail. The radio was dead.

"Stupid batteries," he screamed out loud. "And of course Mr. Bigshot has all the extra batteries in his backpack!" In disgust, Jeremy shoved the useless radio in his back pocket.

Sticking his head through the opened window he yelled out, "You guys? Anybody there? Hello?" There was no answer. Suddenly, the window started to shake. Jeremy jumped back just as it came crashing down, missing his neck by only a few inches. Falling back on his butt, Jeremy looked in disbelief as the latch on the window slowly closed, locking itself from the inside.

"Hey!" he screamed. "My friends are in there!" Jeremy jumped up and tried to force the window open. Pushing with all his might, he gritted his teeth and puffed up his cheeks like a chipmunk. "Arrrrggghhhh ..." he grunted, but the window refused to budge.

Realizing his attempts to pry the window open were futile, Jeremy stepped back and began rubbing his aching wrists. Looking around, he spotted a large rock that looked like it weighed at least five pounds. Hoisting the rock like an Olympic shot-putter, he thrust it forward, using every last muscle in his upper body to send the miniature boulder sailing through the air and straight at the window. But instead of smashing the glass to a million pieces, the rock acted like a tennis ball and simply bounced off the window, rolled to the ground, and came to rest at Jeremy's feet.

"This is insane," Jeremy screamed as he abandoned his attempts to open the window and ran around to the front door.

Inside, everybody was motionless. The air began to get colder and colder. David could see his own breath. Using the radio, he tried frantically to reach Jeremy. There was no answer. Not knowing that the batteries on Jeremy's radio were dead, he yelled into the receiver, "Jeremy you idiot! Why aren't you answering?"

Laura began to shiver as the temperature in the kitchen began to drop to freezing. "We've got to get out of here," She cried. Heading toward the kitchen door, she tried to open it but it wouldn't budge. It was as if someone, or something, were holding it closed.

Carla ran over to help her. Planting their shoulders firmly against the door, the two of them pushed with all their might. Yet the harder they pushed, the harder the door — or whatever was on the other side — pushed back.

"Step back," Laura said. "If this door won't open the old-fashioned way, then I'm going to kick it down!"

"I knew that brown belt would come in handy some day," David smiled as stepped back to give Laura plenty of room.

Standing in perfect position, Laura took a deep breath, focused all of her energy, and using her left leg and foot, gave the door a solid and resounding kick. It flew open. For a moment, everybody was stunned, unsure of what to do next. Suddenly a glass vase flew off a shelf, narrowly missing Austin as it smashed against the wall behind him. He jumped, his notepad and pen flying out of his hands.

"Everybody, out!" David yelled.

Making sure Stinky was firmly tucked in his shirt pocket, Eddie soared through the air as he headed for the open door. Stopping just long enough to pick up his pen and notebook — he would never, in a million years, leave his notes behind — Austin left next. Carla, Laura, and David followed in quick succession.

On the porch, Jeremy was frantically trying to pry open the front door. His hands were now raw and nearly bleeding and his eyes stung from the sweat that poured down his forehead. Without warning, the front door flew open, causing Jeremy to fall forward and smack headlong into Eddie. The collision sent Jeremy flying backwards off the front porch. Barely fazed by the impact, Eddie leapt off the front porch and, with a thud that could be heard for blocks, landed squarely on top of Jeremy.

"Ouch!" Jeremy screamed. "Get off me!"

Eddie quickly rolled off, jumped effortlessly to his feet, and reached into his pocket to make sure Stinky was okay. Stunned but okay, Stinky let out a little squeak that meant he had to pee. Eddie extended his hand to Jeremy, quickly got his friend back on his feet, and immediately released Stinky to do his business.

In a matter of seconds, Austin, Laura, and David joined the others outside.

"Is everybody out?" David asked frantically, as he began to take a head count.

"Carla's not here," Austin yelled. "She's still inside!"

"I'm okay," Carla waved to her friends as she stood just inside the front door. "I had to go back and get that letter Mr. Crankle had been reading just before he died. I got a very strong psychic vibe from it and..."

The front door slammed shut, sealing Carla inside the house. David lunged forward and tried to open it, but the door was now locked. He began pounding on the door, shouting, "Open the door, Carla. Open the door!"

The sound of Carla's screams seeped through the door, "no... please... stay away from me... please, no..." before slowly fading into silence.

CHAPTER 8

ON THE OTHER SIDE

"**C**arla!" Laura yelled as she pounded on the front door, trying frantically to help David pry it open.

"We've got to get help," Austin shouted over the screams of the others. Reaching into his backpack he pulled out his cell phone. As he began to call 911, David grabbed the phone from his hands.

"No, we can't call the police," David tried to explain to a stunned Austin. "We can never let adults know about us. It's the most important rule of the MAC! You know as well as I do that they would never believe us."

"But how do we get Carla back?" Austin asked, as he clutched the cell phone in his hand, his fingers ready to call.

"I'll get her," Jeremy said as he brushed the dirt off his pants. "I'm really ticked off now, and there's no way I'm going to let some freak phantom take my friends hostage!"

David was shocked at his friend's new-found courage. "Jeremy, what are you up to?"

Jeremy pulled his shoulders back and lifted his head high. Running to the front door, he began pounding on it and yelling at the top of his lungs, "Mr. Crankle, I know you're in there! I don't care if you're dead or alive, but I want my friend Carla back...now!" He pounded and yelled for what seemed an eternity, nothing could hold him back.

Just as it seemed Jeremy was going to pound a hole right through the door, the sound of a loud and thunderous crash came from inside the house, sending him reeling backwards a good two feet. He almost slipped off the porch as his left foot came down off the top step.

"What was that?" Austin asked.

David, now standing next to Jeremy, put his hand on his friend's shoulder. The veins in Jeremy forehead were sticking out.

"It's okay, Jeremy," David said, trying to calm his friend down. "Maybe if we try something different? Maybe if we just nicely asked Mr. Crankle to let Carla out?"

"Are you nuts?" Jeremy said, sounding as sarcastic as ever.

"I think David is right," Laura added. "After all, we're the ones who broke into Mr. Crankle's house. We're the intruders. If it were my house, I'd be mad, too."

"But the guy is dead! Why would he care?" The expression on Jeremy's face shifted from frustration to confusion.

David knew better than to continue arguing with Jeremy. At times like this, it was better to stop explaining and do what he thought was right. Clearing his throat and wiping the hair from his eyes, he gave the front door a firm yet respectful knock. As expected, there was no answer.

"Mr. Crankle? Good morning, sir. My name is David Reid, and I'm very sorry we disturbed you. But we were wondering, if you could please let us in so we could get our friend Carla out. We'd really appreciate it. Thank you, sir." David took a deep breath. There was only silence. He looked back at Laura who gave him a nod of encouragement. From the corner of his eye he could see Jeremy snickering.

David continued, "Ah, Mr. Crankle? We're really sorry that we broke into, I mean, that we entered your house without permission, sir."

As a crooked smile slowly spread across his face, Jeremy jumped in, "and we're very sorry to have found you dead, too. That was a total bummer!"

Laura stepped up and gave Jeremy a punch on the shoulder. "What Jeremy meant, sir, is that we're very sorry you passed on. We feel sad that we never had a chance to get to know you better."

"Don't forget to curtsy," Jeremy said as he shot Laura a dirty look. "If you ask me..." the sound of a clicking noise, coming from inside the house, stopped Jeremy mid-sentence.

"What is that?" Laura asked.

"It sounds like somebody is unlocking the door," David answered just in time to witness the front door creak open a few inches then come to a sudden stop.

Laura stepped back then glanced over at David; a look of relief began to appear on his face.

"Carla?" Laura spoke softly, "is that you who opened the door?" There was no answer.

"It's not funny to play tricks on the rest of us, you know!" Jeremy scolded. "Well, you're not scaring me, I want you to know that. I'm coming in, and I'm going to get my friend back."

"You can't go alone," Austin said, as he put his hand on Jeremy's shoulder. "You know it's one of the rules, never enter a haunted house by yourself."

"I won't be alone," Jeremy said. "Carla's in there. Besides, if anything does happen, the rest of you are going to have to get help. It's the only way."

"Don't forget to keep your radio on," David said, gently chiding his friend for not responding when he tried to reach him earlier. "And, if anything happens, call for help."

"I'd be happy to keep my radio on," Jeremy said smugly, "if you wouldn't mind keeping the batteries fully charged!"

David blushed as he reached into his backpack and pulled out a pair of freshly recharged batteries. "Sorry."

"It's okay, dude," Jeremy laughed as he grabbed the batteries and quickly installed them in his radio.

"And remember," Laura added, "if you run into Mr. Crankle, be nice to him and apologize for all the interruptions."

"Yeah, yeah," Jeremy said, sounding like he was talking to his mother, "I'm always nice, remember!"

"Huh!" Eddie grunted from behind.

Ignoring Eddie, Jeremy adjusted his radio and tested it with a "one, two, three." From a few feet away, David used his radio and responded, "I read you, Monster Boy 7. You're ready for action!"

Moving quickly, time was now of the essence, Jeremy didn't bother to look back. Stepping inside the house, he knew he had to find Carla and get her out. Past experience had taught members of the MAC that the longer you spent with an angry dead person, the greater the chance you'd end up a dead person, too.

"Carla?" he called. Like before, there was no answer.

A booming voice suddenly echoed throughout the house, so loud that it could be heard by everybody in the front yard. "Wipe your feet," it commanded.

Jeremy jumped. Without thinking twice he stepped back outside and instinctively began wiping the mud from his favorite pair of trashed sneakers. The others looked shocked by his sudden attention to cleanliness. David laughed to himself, remembering how many times he had heard Jeremy's mother nag him to wipe his feet. And to think, all it took to make him do it was one angry ghost! Jeremy continued wiping his feet for nearly a minute until he was confident there wasn't a trace of dirt left.

"They're clean now, sir," Jeremy said out loud, not exactly sure where he should aim his voice. There was no answer, so he carefully stepped inside the house, glancing back at his tracks to make sure no stray dirt had followed him inside. He was clean.

"Mr. Crankle," he continued, "like my friends said earlier, we're really sorry to have bugged you, and we're very sorry you died, too. But we kind of need your help, sir. Something weird is going on. First my mom got possessed, and then it happened to my sister's teddy bear. We're not saying you had anything to do with it, but, if you could just give us a hint about what's going on, we'd be really grateful. Oh, it would be nice if you'd let us get Carla back, too! And, if there's anything we can do to help you, all you have to do is ask!"

"I'm up here," a voice said, coming from the top of the stairs.

"Carla?" Jeremy was cautious. It sounded like Carla, but something wasn't quite right.

"Come up," the voice called out. "Come upstairs and help me."

"Help you?" Jeremy asked. "Why don't you just come downstairs and we can go home."

"I think I'm on to something," she called down again. "I need your help carrying a box. After all, you're so big and strong!"

Jeremy gulped. The voice sounded like Carla except she would never, in a million years, call him big and strong. His heart was now racing as he slowly climbed the long staircase that led to the second floor of the old house. With each step the wooden staircase creaked.

Carefully pulling the radio from his back pocket, Jeremy radioed an update to David. "Be careful," David radioed back, but the static made it hard for Jeremy to hear.

Jeremy wanted more than anything to turn around and run down the stairs, out the door, and into the safety of the mid-morning sun. But there was no turning back now. For too long members of the MAC had considered him a big chicken. The time had come for Jeremy to prove himself.

As he reached the top of the stairs, Jeremy noticed a light coming from one of the upstairs' rooms. A shadow, much bigger than any shadow Carla could possibly cast, spread across the floor, just beyond the door. If Carla was in there, she wasn't alone.

"I'm here," the voice called again, leading Jeremy toward the room. Now only a step away, Jeremy reached out, and with hardly any effort at all, gave the half-opened door a gentle push. As the door swung open, Jeremy closed his eyes tightly and bit his lower lip.

"Carla?" he called softly, his eyes pinched shut. "I hope that's you standing in front of me!"

Opening one eye just a crack, Jeremy let out a little shriek, took a deep breath, the slowly opened his other eye. The look of terror on his face slowly evaporated into a puzzled expression. In front of him stood a little old lady. Her head was bent down and it made it difficult to see her face. A large gray shawl covered her stooped shoulders and a pair of reading glasses hung from a gold chain around her neck. Her right arm was outstretched revealing a hand that was all wrinkled. Her fingers, like the claws on a giant bird, were crooked and bent. She was silent, almost as if she were unaware of Jeremy's presence.

"Excuse me, Ma'am," Jeremy said softly, not wanting to startle her. "I'm sorry to bug you, but I'm looking for my friend, Carla. I thought I heard her calling from upstairs."

Without lifting her head, the old woman spoke. "I'm here," she said. The hairs on Jeremy's neck bristled. The voice he heard coming from the old woman sounded just like Carla's voice. But how could that be? Jeremy began to stagger. Sweat beaded on his forehead and the palms of his hands became clammy.

"But you're not Carla," he stammered. "You can't be Carla."

"But I am," she said, still looking away. "Jeremy, you've got to help me. Mr. Crankle needs to be with his wife before it's too late. She's been waiting for him you know. All this time."

Jeremy swallowed hard. "Okay," he said, "we can do that, sure."

"And Jeremy," the old woman continued, still sounding like Carla, "Mrs. Crankle is very sad.

Nobody was here to keep an eye on her husband. He died, all by himself. He was alone, Jeremy."

"I'm sorry ..." Jeremy's voice trailed off.

"Make it right, Jeremy. You and your friends have to make it right. And if you don't ..." the old woman suddenly became silent.

"Yes?" Jeremy asked, breathless as his voice trembled.

"If you don't," she said, "Carla will spend the rest of eternity with me!"

The old woman lifted her head and Jeremy found himself staring into the empty eye sockets of a skeleton. He screamed!

"Make it right, Jeremy," she screeched like a witch, all traces of Carla's voice now gone. "You have one hour to bring Edmund to me... or Carla is never coming back!"

Then suddenly she was gone. In her place lay the letter that Carla had originally gone back to get. Grabbing the letter, Jeremy stuffed it in his pocket, bolted down the stairs, burst through the front door and, once outside, began tearing down the street like a wounded rabbit running for cover from a very hungry fox.

CHAPTER 9

THE LETTER

Running as fast as humanly possible, Jeremy's feet barely touched the ground. David, Laura, and the rest of the MAC followed in close pursuit, all the while yelling for him to stop.

"Hey, slow down... stop..." David screamed as his legs throbbed to keep up.

Reaching the safety of his own house, Jeremy came to a sudden stop in the front yard. Falling to his knees and grabbing his aching sides, he struggled to catch his breath as he choked the words out, one at a time, "Carla... trouble... gone... forever... unless... help... Edmund... died... alone... get... together... one hour... now!"

Laura, her extensive ballet training having made her a top athlete, was hardly winded at all. She sat down next to Jeremy, placed her hand on his shoulder, and did her best to interpret. "I think what he's trying to say," she continued, "is that we need to somehow reunite Mr. and Mrs. Crankle, or else Carla is never coming back from the other side. And we have one hour to do it. Is that correct?"

"Yes!" Jeremy screamed before falling flat on his face.

It took another five minutes before Jeremy recovered enough to tell the others in detail what had happened. As he spoke, the familiar sound of "Stars and Stripes" could be heard coming from down the street. In a matter of minutes the 4th of July parade would be only a block away.

Trying to make sense of what was happening, David listened to every word Jeremy uttered. "The old woman you saw," he asked, "do you think that could have been Mrs. Crankle?"

"She looks like this," Austin said as he unfolded the yellowed newspaper obituary with Mrs. Crankle's picture on it.

"I think that was her," Jeremy said. "It's hard to imagine what she'd look like as a skeleton. Wait a minute," Jeremy was excited, "the glasses."

"What glasses?" Eddie asked as he took Stinky out of his pocket and began to pet him.

"In the picture, she's wearing glasses on a gold chain. Those were the same glass and the same gold chain the skeleton had around her neck."

"So it was Mrs. Crankle! Good detective work," Laura said to Jeremy as she helped him back on his feet.

"But this doesn't make sense," David said, thinking back to the conversation he and his mother had about the Crankle's. "According to my mother, Mrs. Crankle was a teacher who loved kids. Why would she all of a sudden want to kidnap Carla?"

"Because," Laura offered, "she's hurt."

Jeremy looked confused. "Hurt? She's more than hurt, she's dead!"

"No, you idiot," Laura said. "I meant that her feelings were hurt. Think how you would feel if the person you loved more than anyone in the world died alone, and nobody even noticed."

"Well I wouldn't go around kidnapping other people's kids, that's for sure!" Jeremy responded, his eyes narrowing with anger as he spoke. "Besides, if she's dead, and he's dead, what's the big deal? Why can't they just hang out together where all the other mean old dead people hang out?!"

"Maybe Mr. Crankle doesn't know he's dead yet?" Eddie spoke softly, sounding unsure if what he was saying would make any sense to the others.

Austin tilted his head to one side as his nose started twitching, a sign that he was in deep thought. David looked at Eddie, exchanged a knowing glance with Laura, then looked back to Eddie once again. "You know, Eddie," he said, "you just may be on to something."

"Really?" Eddie sounded surprised that the others were actually considering his theory as plausible.

"What do people who are in love want more than anything in the world?" Austin asked.

"To smooch 24 hours a day!' Jeremy laughed.

"You know, for being such a jerk, you're pretty close," Laura jumped in. "People who are in love want to be together, forever."

"Right," Austin agreed, "and for some reason, even though Mr. and Mrs. Crankle are now both dead, and presumably could be together, they're not? But why?"

"Because," Eddie jumped in, "Mr. Crankle doesn't know that he's dead?!"

"Somehow," David continued, "we have to tell Mr. Crankle that he's dead and help him find his wife on the other side."

Jeremy could only snicker. "No problem, chief. And when we're done with that, maybe we can host a big anniversary party in their honor!"

"Researchers tell us," Laura said as she ignored Jeremy, "that most ghosts haunt places because they are somehow trapped between the world of the living and the world of the dead, never knowing that they've actually died."

"So wait a minute," Jeremy jumped in, his voice sounding confused, "you mean to say that

Mr. Crankle, that smelly old decomposing guy on the kitchen floor, doesn't know he's dead? And until he knows he's dead, he can't be with Mrs. Crankle? What does he need, a GPS?!"

"Not a GPS," David said, "just somebody to guide him across to the other side."

"No problem!" Jeremy said as he began wiping the loose grass blades off his dirty jeans. "And if we walk Mr. Crankle to the land of the dead in the next fifteen minutes, we'll all be back in plenty of time to catch the parade! That is, if we come back at all?! What, are you people all nuts?!"

David just shook his head, but deep down, he knew Jeremy was right. Once they helped Mr. Crankle cross over, and hopefully reunited him with Mrs. Crankle, there would be no guarantee that any of them would be able to cross back to the land of the living.

"What's that in your pocket?" Eddie asked, noticing the letter that Jeremy had grabbed just before he bolted from the house.

"The skeleton lady was holding it," Jeremy explained. "When she disappeared, it was all that was left."

"That must have been the letter that Carla went back to get," David said, as he took the letter from Jeremy, unfolded it, and read it slowly to himself.

Turning around, David began walking.

"Where are you going?" Jeremy yelled after him.

"Back to Mr. And Mrs. Crankle's house," David said as he turned back to face the group. "Somebody has to figure out how to reunite Mr. And Mrs. Crankle and rescue Carla."

"But how?" Eddie asked.

"I'm pretty sure," David said, "the answer is in this letter." And with that, he turned on his heels and began heading back to the Crankle's house.

CHAPTER 10

THE SPEED DEMON OF BAYVIEW CENTRAL

As the sun rose higher in the sky, the late morning heat was beginning to take its toll on Kimmy and the rest of the parade participants. Whether they were marching, riding atop one of the red, white and blue decorated floats, or on their bikes like Kimmy, virtually everyone in the 4th of July parade was glowing with a sticky sweat. The humidity that was so much a part of every Bayview summer seemed even worse when the downtown streets and sidewalks were so crowded.

Kimmy navigated her bike carefully, constantly monitoring the riders in front and behind her. One wrong move and it would be an instant pile-up of bikes. It had happened once before, long before she had been born. Before the day's parade had begun, Mr. Dorsey, the man in charge of everything, reminded the bike riders about "The 1995 Great 4th of July Parade Pileup" as he liked to call it. He talked about the skinned and bloody knees in such graphic detail that three of the younger bikers backed out and two more were dragged out, kicking and screaming, by their overprotective parents.

"What little babies," Kimmy said to the girl next to her.

Kimmy had never been afraid of a little challenge, and certainly riding her bike in the annual 4th of July Parade was worth every risk. Still, as the heat began to take its toll, the excitement of being in the parade was quickly fading. Soon Kimmy would be riding past Bayview Realty, where her parents worked, and would need to smile and wave as her father took pictures. But after she had passed them on the parade route, it would be so easy to swerve off, down the side street, and over to the Crankle's house where the rest of the MAC had gone that morning.

Watching her father look at pictures he had taken of her on his brand new camera, Kimmy made her move. One of the other kids noticed her exit and cried out to a parade monitor, but the confused adult in the yellow vest couldn't hear a thing over the noise of the crowd. Within a few seconds Kimmy, the undisputed speed demon of

Bayview Central Second Grade, was out of sight and on her way to the Crankle's house.

As she rode closer to the house, the sounds of the parade quickly faded away. The Crankle's house slipped into view and she began looking for the others' bikes, hidden in bushes or behind the huge oak trees that lined the sleepy street. Her eyes searched but she saw nothing.

"Hey guys," she yelled, "it's me. Where are you hiding?"

But the only answer in return was the sound of a blue jay squawking loudly from the trees above.

Double-checking that none of the neighbors were watching, Kimmy parked her bike behind some overgrown bushes, out of sight from the street. In the patches of dry dirt that ran along the side of the Crankle's house, she stopped to look at fresh footprints that were scattered in several directions.

"So you guys were here," she said out loud, the sound of her own voice was somehow comforting. "I wonder why you all left?" she continued to herself, almost sounding like she expected an answer.

As she slowly walked around the house and past the side window, a sudden movement from inside the house caught her attention. Tiptoeing cautiously to the side of the window, she craned her neck to peek inside. There was nobody there.

"Kimmy," the voice was soft and gentle, but it startled Kimmy, and she let out a scream.

"Who's there?" Kimmy asked, jumping back from the window.

"It's me...Carla. You've come for me, Kimmy." Carla said, her voice sounding very distant.

"Carla," Kimmy said, "if it is you, you sound a little strange right now. And how come I can hear you, but I can't see you?"

"I'm on the other side, Kimmy. Open the window, and come join me."

"The other side," Kimmy gulped. "You mean the other side of the house?"

"No," Carla sounded very serious, "the other side of life. I'm in a place where dead people go after they die. Where they go to finish things."

"Finish things?" Kimmy repeated. "Finish what?"

"Lots of things," Carla called back, a hint of excitement filling her voice. "Things they weren't able to finish on earth. Things they need to get done before they can truly move on."

"Sounds kind of creepy to me!" Kimmy said, her voice getting louder.

"It's not creepy," Carla said, "but it can be very sad. All the dead people here are trapped, not able to go all the way over because of something unfinished in our world."

"Wow!" Kimmy said. "I guess I know why you guys never wanted me to join the MAC. All this dead stuff is kind of freaky, you know. Hey, you're not...you're not dead, are you?"

"Come join me," Carla said again, this time her voice sounding more urgent.

"I guess I can," Kimmy called back as she placed her hands on the ledge of the window and, with little effort, pushed it open. "Oh hey, I can give you your grandmother's beads, too. Remember the amulet you gave me? The one that you said would protect me from evil spirits? Sounds like you might need it more than I do!"

"No amulets, Kimmy," Carla cried. "What we need to do is help Mr. Crankle. That's why Mrs. Crankle brought us here."

As Kimmy pulled herself up onto the ledge and began to pull her body through the open window, a much deeper voice entered the conversation.

"So it was Mrs. Crankle that brought us here!"

Kimmy flinched, startled by the sudden voice behind her. Jumping off the window ledge, she swung around, ready to give the intruder a painful kick.

"Back off, or I'm going to kick you where it counts," she screamed before realizing the other voice was coming from David. He and the rest of the MAC had snuck up behind her and were now listening in astonishment to everything Carla was saying.

"Hey, you guys!" Kimmy squealed with excitement. "Boy, am I glad to see you!"

"You just couldn't mind your own business, could you?" Jeremy said, deepening his voice to sound like his father. Instead, he sounded just like an older brother who was annoyed beyond belief.

"Ah, shut up, you big jerk. I was doing just fine communicating with Carla. Besides, she's on the other side, you know?"

"Yeah, we know!" Jeremy snapped back, refusing to give any credit to his little sister.

"Shhhh ..." David ordered, "We can't lose contact with Carla!"

"Carla? It's me, Laura. Are you still there?"

There was a moment of silence before Carla spoke again. As she did, everyone sighed with relief.

"I'm here, Laura. But something strange is starting to happen."

"What's happening?" David shouted, trying not to sound as panicked as he was now feeling.

There was a long pause, then Carla spoke again. Only this time the tone of her voice was becoming more serious, darker. "I think we're running out of time. The doorway that leads from this world to our world is starting to close. And

I'm afraid if we don't help Mr. and Mrs. Crankle soon, I'm going to be trapped here ... forever!"

"But how do we help them?" Eddie screamed from behind David. "Tell us?"

But this time there was no reply.

"Everybody, we've got to work together. I need each of you to read this letter and see if it offers any clues," David said, as he unfolded the letter and shared it with the others.

"That's the same letter I read inside the house," Laura said, as she scanned the piece of paper held firmly in David's hands. "From the clues inside the house, that was one of the last letters Mr. Crankle was reading before he died."

"Judging from the number of love letters Mr. Crankle wrote his wife over the years, they were very much in love, correct?" Austin asked, already using his scientific mind to try and find the answers.

"Yes, Dr. Love," Jeremy croaked, "so what's your point?"

David was about to let Jeremy have it, when all of a sudden a sentence in the letter made him think about his own parents.

"Each day I caress the wedding ring that binds us together and from it, gather the strength to go on."

The sentence reminded David how, when his parents had divorced, they told him although they weren't in love anymore, their love for him would never change. He remembered how they had each removed their wedding rings and had decided to combine the metals and stones to make a ring that they would give to David on his 18th birthday. At the time it had all seemed so confusing. But now, David was beginning to understand. His parents' love for each other had been symbolized in their rings. And even though that love had changed, and no longer existed as it once had, it ultimately produced a much greater love, their love for their son. And the rings, now combined into a single ring and stored away until David's 18th birthday, were the symbol of that new and greater love.

"We need to get Mr. Crankle's wedding ring and bring it to Mrs. Crankle," David said, confident that he now understood. "Once it's there, I'm certain Mr. Crankle will follow."

"Follow where?" Austin asked.

"To Mrs. Crankle's grave. If we can get the ring and place it on her grave, my hunch is that he'll follow. And once he's there, he'll realize that he now belongs there, resting eternally next to his wife."

"And once he's resting eternally, he can stop haunting Bayview!" Jeremy exclaimed.

"Except he's not the one haunting Bayview," Laura offered.

Jeremy was now confused. "Huh?"

"Don't you see? All this time it's been Mrs. Crankle. It was her way of getting our attention. Her way of asking us to help guide Mr. Crankle back to the other side."

"Well it sure got my attention," Jeremy snickered. "As long as my mom stays my mom, and Mr. Boggles stays in the garbage with all the other trashed toys, then I'm happy to do whatever it takes to bring Mr. and Mrs. Crankle together."

"Great," David smiled, "then you don't mind going back in the house and getting the wedding ring? If I remember correctly, it rolled next to Mr. Crankle's body."

"Are you nuts?" Jeremy's eyes bugged wide. "I don't care what you guys say about me, there's no way I'm going back in that house to pick up some dead guy's ring! No way!"

"Stinky can do it," Eddie offered, sounding unsure of what he was offering.

"Are you sure?" David asked. "This could be a dangerous mission, Eddie. There's every chance Stinky might not make it out alive."

Eddie swallowed hard. "I'm sure. Stinky's brave enough to do this," Eddie said as he wiped a small tear from the corner of his eye.

"Eddie's right. There's no point in sending a boy to do a hamster's job," Laura cracked as she gave Jeremy a spiteful look.

Grabbing hold of Jeremy's sleeve, Austin pulled his red-faced friend back. "Besides, I need your help. While they're getting the ring, you and I need to head to the cemetery see if we can find the exact location of Mrs. Crankle's grave. Hopefully someone will be working in the office and can help us find it."

"Good idea," David agreed. Double-checking the time, he continued, "it's exactly 10:40 a.m. right now, and we only have 50 minutes left, or we'll be too late. We'll plan to meet up with the two of you at the entrance to Oaks Cemetery at exactly 11:05 a.m. If all goes right, we should be able to drop off the ring, reunite Mr. and Mrs. Crankle, and get Carla back by noon, before our parents start getting suspicious."

A growling sound came from Jeremy's stomach. "And most important, we'll be back in plenty of time for the town's 1:00 pm barbeque!"

Eddie rolled his eyes as Jeremy and Austin retrieved their bikes and headed to the Oaks Cemetery to begin their search for Mrs. Crankle's grave. Reaching into his pocket, he pulled out Stinky, sound asleep and very annoyed at suddenly being woken up. "It's okay little guy. Sorry to disturb you," Eddie gently stroked the fur on Stinky's neck. "But we've got one more assignment. And this one's a doozey."

Stretching, his little hamster mouth wide open in what looked like a huge yawn followed by the shaking of his chubby hamster butt, Stinky was now ready for action. His nose twitching back and forth, Stinky looked Eddie straight in the eyes, then scurried down his leg.

David looked on in fascination as Eddie, now clearly communicating with Stinky through some sort of mental telepathy that was hard to comprehend, guided his little friend through the open window and back into the house where Mr. Crankle's wedding ring lay waiting.

Clearly in a trance, Eddie spoke out loud as he guided Stinky onward. "Ok, little buddy, a couple more feet to the right, through the kitchen door, yes that's it. Good. Okay, that's him right there. I know, it's kind of smelly. Ok, now remember the ring you had in your mouth? Yeah, the gold band. Now it fell somewhere on the floor so I need you to look real carefully for it. Is that it? It looks like ... nope, that's just a cap from a soda bottle. Keep looking. To the right ... yeah, I think I see something too. It's on the floor, right next to Mr. Crankle's hand. That's it. Okay, now be very careful ... careful ... okay, good. Now put it in your mouth ... good boy! Now carefully carry it back out the way you came in. Wait ... Stinky where are you going? Cheese? On the floor? Yeah, I guess you can have a bite ... no wait, stop! That's not cheese, it's a mouse trap! If you go after the cheese, that metal thing is going to snap and break your neck. Yeah, I know! It's very gross. Ok, I promise I'll buy you some cheese when you come out. Yes, I'll make sure it's cheddar, your favorite. Come on, Stinky, back through the door, up the ledge, and right back through the open window ..."

The rest of the MAC watched in amazement as, sure enough, Stinky came bounding back through the open window, Mr. Crankle's wedding ring clenched firmly in his little hamster mouth.

"Three cheers for Stinky and Eddie," Kimmy cried out, and the rest of the members of the MAC quickly obliged. Eddie smiled broadly as Stinky crawled up his arm and deposited the golden ring in his outstretched hand.

"Good job," David said, as he gave his friend a pat on the shoulder, and carefully wrapped the ring inside a handkerchief. "Ok everybody, now that we've got the ring, we've got to hurry and get to the cemetery."

As he jumped on his bike, Stinky now safely resting back inside his front pocket, Eddie called to David, "On our way there, can we stop at the store and buy Stinky his cheese?"

"We don't have enough time," David yelled back as he mounted his bike. "But don't worry, on the way back, we're going to stop at the store and buy Stinky 10 lbs of the best cheddar cheese money can buy!"

CHAPTER 11

AT THE CEMETERY

The late morning sun was blocked out by the large grove of oak trees that stood guard over the thousands of graves that filled up Bayview's only cemetery. For such a small town it was a huge graveyard, one that seemed to sprawl for several acres in every direction. Unless Austin and Jeremy were able to find the exact location of Mrs. Crankle's grave, it would be almost impossible to randomly locate it by reading the inscription on each and every headstone. Just getting through the first section alone could take many hours.

It had taken David and the other members of the MAC less than 10 minutes to get to the entrance of the cemetery. It was now a few minutes past the agreed rendezvous time, and still there was no sign of either Jeremy or Austin. David was getting anxious, wondering if he should have sent Laura to help Austin instead of Jeremy. David knew that they didn't have much time left to find the grave, return the ring, and retrieve Carla from the other side.

"Hey!" It was Jeremy, his face red and sweaty, as he struggled to balance on the back of Austin's bike. "My bike blew a tire, so I had to hitch a ride from Austin!"

"Did you find it?" David sounded impatient.

"Sure did, chief!"

David hated it when Jeremy called him "chief," but now was not the time to bring it up. Instead, he smiled broadly and congratulated Austin and Jeremy on their good detective work.

Austin mumbled a faint "thanks" before motioning for the others to follow him. As they rode their bikes on the narrow dirt roads that crisscrossed the cemetery, David found himself amazed at the variety of gravestones they passed.

The last time he had come to the cemetery was to visit his grandmother's grave. Although David had never met his grandmother, she had died before he was even born, he always felt an overwhelming sadness every time he visited her grave. His mother would tell him stories about what a great woman she had been, and David felt himself feeling almost angry that he had never had a chance to know her. If only he had been born earlier. Or, if only she had lived longer!

"Look at that one," Eddie called out as he passed a grave, marked by a very large statue of a woman that looked just like the hundreds of ancient statues they had once seen on a field trip to the Chicago Art Museum. Underneath the statue, carefully engraved on a gravestone, was the name of the woman who was buried there along with her birth and death dates. Much of the engraving had worn down over the years and was difficult to read. Coming to a stop, Eddie strained to make out the woman's name. "Wow," he exclaimed, "that woman, Mrs. Reynolds, was 19 when she died. And she's been dead for over a hundred years!"

"That's fascinating," Jeremy called from ahead. "Unfortunately, we'll have to take the cemetery tour some other time! Keep peddling!"

Eddie shrugged, got back on his bike, and peddled double-time to catch up. As they moved up the narrow roads, wide enough for no more that two bikes or a single car, David noticed that the gravestones were becoming smaller, the trees not as tall, and that the dates of people's deaths were much more recent.

"We're getting close," Austin yelled out as he slowed his bike down. "This is the newer section of the cemetery, and according to the map in the office, Mrs. Crankle was buried ten years ago in this area."

Hopping off the back of Austin's bike, Jeremy ran off the path and instinctively headed to a grave as if he had been there a million times before. "It should be right ... there! There it is!" Jeremy was almost jumping up and down as he pointed at the small marble slab that marked Mrs. Crankle's grave. It was not nearly as fancy as some of the other grave markers they had seen that day. Still, when David read the inscription out loud, it sent chills down his spine.

Charlotte Crankle, Loving Wife
July 4, 1927 – May 23, 2004

Edwin Crankle, Loving Husband
April 12, 1922 –

Beloved Educators
Friends To Countless Children

"Today was Mrs. Crankle's birthday," Laura observed.

"Yeah," Eddie nodded, "and look, there's no death date for Mr. Crankle."

"Yet," Jeremy added.

"So they were both teachers," David added, ignoring Jeremy.

"What do you mean?" Eddie asked.

"My mom had talked about Mrs. Crankle being a teacher. She never mentioned that Mr. Crankle had also been a teacher. But look, the tombstone mentions how they were both 'educators' and 'friends' to all these kids."

"So all this time," Laura said as she gazed down at the gravestone, one of the few that had no fresh flowers, "people always thought Mr. Crankle was this mean, terrible old man who hated kids. Nobody took the time to get to know him and find out the truth."

A slight smile spread across Austin's face. "Now we do know the truth. And when this is all over, we can go about setting the record straight."

As David pulled the ring, still carefully wrapped up in a handkerchief, out of his pocket, a cold wind came sweeping through the cemetery. Out of place on such a warm and muggy July morning, the wind was so intense that for a moment David felt he was going to be blown backwards. The ring, held firmly in his clenched hand, suddenly blew free. David watched in horror as the gold band gave flight, sweeping back and forth on the tail of the forceful wind before landing next to the Crankle's gravestone. Then, as quickly as it came, the wind disappeared, leaving battered leaves and twisted branches in its wake.

Instinctively, David reached down to retrieve the ring. Just as he grabbed it, someone – or something – grabbed him in return. A hand, covered with fresh dirt and crawling with earthworms, had shot out of the grave and wrapped its fingers around David's wrist. He struggled to pull free but the grip around his wrist was too tight. Someone from inside the grave had taken hold and wasn't about to let go. The grip was so tight that David felt as if he were going to be pulled down into the grave.

"Help me!" he screamed. Jumping up, Laura wrapped her arms around David's waist and began pulling with all her might. Forming a human chain, the other members of the MAC —even Jeremy — lined up behind her. In spite of their combined effort, whatever had hold of David's hand was stronger.

The hand had now completely disappeared under the earth, pulling most of David's arm with it. David's face was now flush with the earth and he was choking on the dirt that had found its way into his mouth. He was terrified that either his arm would literally be ripped from its socket or his whole body was going to be sucked into the muddy earth below. And then, as suddenly as it all started, the thing that had hold of David stopped pulling. The other members of the MAC fell backward, landing with a thump on the freshly mowed lawn.

David yanked his arm out. His fingers and wrist were numb and his arm muscles ached as if he had just done 100 chin-ups in a row. As intense as the pain was, it instantly vanished as soon as David realized the ring was gone. Mrs. Crankle — at least he assumed it was Mrs. Crankle — had literally pulled it out of his hand and taken it to her grave.

"Are you okay?" Laura asked, still shaking from the experience.

"I'm fine," the voice replied. Only it wasn't David's voice they heard. It was Carla's. She was standing quietly behind them, as if she had been there all the time.

"Carla!" Jeremy seemed the most excited of all to see his friend. Without even pausing, he jumped up and gave her a huge hug. Hesitant at first, Carla finally gave in and hugged Jeremy back.

"Are you ok?" Laura asked, her arm placed firmly around Carla's shoulders.

"I'm fine. Really. It's strange," she said, "all that time, while you guys were frantically running around, Mrs. Crankle and I just talked."

"Talked? About what?" Jeremy asked, his mouth wide open.

"About how much she loved Mr. Crankle, and about how sad she was that nobody had been there to keep an eye out for him and make sure he was okay. And we talked about a lot of woman stuff, too."

"Things that you would never understand!" Laura added, as she pushed Jeremy aside and gave Carla a little wink.

"Try me!" Jeremy protested.

"The important thing," Carla said, changing the subject and sounding unusually calm for a person who had just spent so much time talking with a dead person, "is that now they're together. As scary as Mrs. Crankle made things sound, deep down, I knew I was never in danger. It was her only way to get our attention and help Mr. Crankle cross over."

"And what about our mom," Jeremy asked, putting his arm around Kimmy who pushed him away. "Is she going to be okay?"

"Yes," Carla explained "your mom is going to be fine, and she won't have any memory of what happened. When you and Kimmy played your little prank on her, Mrs. Crankle saw it as the perfect way to get our attention."

"Next time, tell her to just write a note!" Jeremy said, sounding as sarcastic as ever.

Helping Carla get on the back of Laura's bike, Austin smiled at his friend. "Good job," he said.

As the members of the MAC rode silently out of the cemetery, David could sense that there were hundreds of eyes that were watching them. He looked at his watch. It was now nearly 11:30. If they hurried back and cleaned up, they could make the town's barbeque in plenty of time. And, as was standard MAC protocol, none of the adults in Bayview would ever have to know about their most unusual 4th of July.

CHAPTER 12

NEVER ALONE

On July 8th a small article appeared in the local newspaper. Without going into too much detail, it said that the police, responding to an anonymous call, discovered the body of an elderly man in his residence on Third Street.

According to the story, the county medical examiner indicated that the man, identified as Mr. Edwin Crankle, had died of natural causes and estimated the time of death as Sunday, July 2nd. In his case file, David noted that the reported date of death corresponded to the day when all the paranormal activity first began.

The story went on to say that the police assumed that the anonymous call came from some mischievous kids who had probably broken into the house. The article quoted the Chief of Police, "Those kids, we think there were at least four of them based on the number of footprints we found outside the house, were playing some kind of prank. They got a lot more than they bargained for when they came upon the body. My guess is they won't be breaking into anymore houses anytime soon!"

As he reread the article and carefully scanned it for his files, David was struck not by what it said, but by what it didn't say. Nowhere in the article did it talk about Mr. Crankle's life and the impact he had made on so many kids. Deep down David knew that the town of Bayview had somehow let Mr. Crankle down. Sitting down at his computer, David began to write a letter to the editor of the local newspaper.

Dear Editor:

This past week the town of Bayview lost a very important citizen. To most people he was just an old man who wanted to live alone. But deep down, he was much more than that. He was a teacher who had dedicated his life to helping kids learn and become better people. He was also a husband who loved his wife very much. If more people had taken the time to know Mr. Crankle when he was alive, perhaps he would not have been so lonely and misunderstood these past few years.

I wonder how many more people just like Mr. Crankle are living in our town right now. Mr. Crankle died alone. As sad as his death was, hopefully it will remind all of us to be more kind to our neighbors.

Sincerely,
David Reid, 6th Grader (as of September), Bayview Central

The letter was published on the day of Mr. Crankle's memorial service. Over 30 of his former students from downstate, now all adults and many with kids of their own, showed up to pay respect. Of course, David and his mother, and all the members of the MAC were there as well. A copy of David's letter had been placed in the church next to Mr. And Mrs. Crankle's wedding picture.

When David got home, he rushed to his bedroom to quickly change into a pair of shorts before heading back out. His mother, getting ready to go back to work, stopped him as he opened the front door. "I didn't realize you had gotten to know so much about Mr. Crankle. Your letter was quite beautiful, honey."

But David, barely having time to blush, was already halfway out the door.

"Where are you going?" his Mother called after him.

"To say 'Hi' to Mrs. Johnson across the street," he said. "I haven't seen her in a while, and I just want to let her know that we're here for her, just in case she ever needs anything. Besides, who knows how many great stories she might have about growing up in the olden days? Or better yet, really good ghost stories!"

"You know I don't believe in ghosts," his mother called after him. But David was already gone.

Suddenly a voice, so quiet that it was hard to hear, seemed to call out, "Be proud of your son, he's a fine young man." Mrs. Reid turned back to where she thought the voice was coming from, but no one was there.

"Hmmm ..." she said to herself, "must have just been the wind blowing through the trees, or maybe it was just the stray sounds from the neighbor's television set." Then, picking up her briefcase and her car keys as she prepared to head out, she turned around and, to no one at all, said, "I'm not sure if anyone is there, but if you are, I agree with you completely; I do have a wonderful son."

Across the street, Mr. And Mrs. Crankle watched Mrs. Johnson's eyes light up at the sight of the young neighbor who had come just to say 'Hi.' Nobody could see Mr. and Mrs. Crankle, of course, and they knew that these would be their last memories in Bayview; it was now time for them to move on to the other side and never look back. Stealing one last moment, they watched as Mrs. Johnson opened her arms and invited David inside her house to have a piece of freshly-baked cherry pie.

And then Mr. And Mrs. Crankle were gone. Even though they would never be returning to the place they had called home for so many years, there was no sadness. They would never be alone again.

The End

ABOUT THE AUTHOR

JL lives with his family, including two rescue dogs and a rescue kitty, in a really old house just outside of San Francisco, CA. He's not sure if the house is haunted, but sometimes he hears weird noises in the middle of the night and wonders what his pets are staring at in the hallway. JL has published all kinds of things for adults and kids, but likes writing scary stories most of all. Sometimes he sleeps with the lights on.

The Monsters' Anonymous Club return in their newest adventure: The Ghoul Gallery!

For more information and to read excerpts from the new book, be sure to follow J.L. Lipp on Facebook at
www.facebook.com/J.L.Lipp

41062604R00079

Made in the USA
Lexington, KY
28 April 2015